D1569089

G.B. Gurland has been an educator for over forty years. She has extensive experience working with school-age children, adolescents, and young adults with reading and literacy challenges. More recently she has turned her attention to writing children's books, and has edited and published several workbooks in the area of vocabulary development. *The Secret Files of Phineas Foster* is her first middle grade novel.

For Emily, Rebecca and Zachary

G. B. Gurland

The Secret Files of
Phineas Foster

AUSTIN MACAULEY
PUBLISHERS LTD.

A CIP catalogue record for this title is available from the British Library.

ISBN 9781786293329 (Paperback)
ISBN 9781786293336 (Hardback)
ISBN 9781786293343 (E-Book)
www.austinmacauley.com

First Published (2016)
Austin Macauley Publishers Ltd.
25 Canada Square
Canary Wharf
London
E14 5LQ

My sincere gratitude to those who believed in the story, encouraged me to write it, and trusted me enough to read it. I would like to thank the children, some now all grown up, who laughed in all of the right places, questioned me when things did not quite make sense, and prodded me for the next installment, Tsvi, Alexa, Jacob, Shaina, Amanda, and Noah. My appreciation and deepest respect for all of the wonderfully creative people I've met through Gotham Writers Workshop and the Society for Children's Book Writers and Illustrators, Harriet Alonso, Lizzie Ross, Laurin Grollman, and Joe Nagler. Their generosity and commitment to children's writing continue to inspire me. I am indebted to family, friends, and colleagues who read, commented, and advised me along the way, Bradley and Lauren Adler, Sharon Modell, Bob Scherma, Susan Bohne, Leda and Michael Molly, Lisa Gilman, and Dorothy Varon. I could never have brought Gabe, Alex, and Phineas to the page without the unwavering love and support of my teacher, mentor, and personal guru, Beryl Adler.

Contents

Chapter One

Encounter at Thirty-Five Thousand Feet

Gabriel raced through the crowded airport terminal. He could barely keep up with his mother who seemed to be trying to break an Olympic record for some yet to be discovered athletic event. "Do you have your homework? Did you remember to pack your summer reading? You didn't forget it, did you?" she inquired, almost completely out of breath.

Try as he might to forget this intrusion, Gabriel did not forget his summer homework on pain of death by talking. His mother would have gone on endlessly about his lack of responsibility, and if she spared him, his father certainly would have finished him off.

Gabriel's reputation was pretty well established. Maybe it was the mop of reddish blond hair that always seemed in need of cutting. Maybe it was the bewildered expression that accompanied any adult's request. Gabriel understood he was viewed as a stubborn almost teenager who very rarely did anything right. The verdict was in, and he knew it. What's more, he didn't think there was much he could do to change people's minds.

Tall for his age, and as a result usually taken for an older child, Gabe, which most everyone except his teachers called him, knew every trick for getting through school with the least possible effort. But he knew enough not to mess with summer homework or his visits with his father whom he saw only three times a year would be plagued with warnings and guilt.

Arriving at the gate with no time to spare, Gabe boarded the jet reluctantly. He looked forward to the time with his dad, but dreaded the thought of flying. This had pretty much been the arrangement since his parents' divorce two years earlier. Transcontinental flights three times a year—winter recess, spring break, and of course summer vacation. In the past his mother had escorted him on these trips, but at age twelve and seven eighths, with thirteen rapidly approaching this summer, his parents had agreed that he could make this voyage solo. He did, however, have the help of the doting flight attendant who walked him to his seat, checked to make sure he was securely fastened, and made certain that his electronic devices were turned off and carefully stowed for take-off.

He didn't plan to speak to anyone on the plane, hoping to have the row to himself or to be sitting next to a monk who had taken a vow of silence. He closed his eyes praying for sleep, or at least praying whoever sat next to him would think he was asleep. Through the narrow slit opening of his pretending-to-sleep eyes, he observed the flight attendants close the overhead bins and prepare the cabin for take-off. Gabe breathed a louder than he realized sigh of relief, as the two seats in his row remained empty. He was in the clear, or so he thought.

"Sorry, young man, but this gentleman was seated in a row where he would have to assist other passengers in the event of an emergency," the flight attendant whispered to the apparently napping Gabe.

With that she carefully positioned a very old and odd-looking man on the aisle of Gabe's row, leaving one seat between the two passengers. *Assist other passengers*, Gabe thought to himself as he glanced briefly at the old man. This guy was barely conscious. Well at least it was not very likely that he would do much talking.

Now about twenty minutes into the flight, the plane seemed to be wrestling with the clouds as it climbed above a storm. Not a very comfortable feeling for a reluctant passenger. For a moment Gabe actually wanted someone to talk to; even this old geezer might offer him some comfort. The fact was, he was simply terrified of heights and flying, and the likelihood of five hours of turbulent skies was not a very happy thought as the plane took off from LAX in Los Angeles. Destination — JFK in New York City and a rather boring drive out to eastern Long Island with his father's driver.

Despite giving it his best shot, Gabe couldn't sleep. The food tasted like marinated cardboard. He barely could move his legs in the cramped seat. And forget the movie. It was impossible to see the screen with the block and tackle passing up and down the aisles between the flight attendants and the passengers to and from the miniature bathrooms. It was simple. Flying was not Gabe's thing.

No matter what he tried to do, it was going to be five hours of torture. He couldn't find a useful distraction; his nerves were a wreck, and the bumpy battle between the plane and the clouds continued. He looked out of the window and hoped for clear skies. But no such luck.

Then at thirty-five thousand feet, Gabe heard a soft gravelly voice from the aisle seat. "My name, my name is Phineas Foster," said the speaker somewhat cautiously.

Okay, Gabe thought, *a talker after all.* He didn't really want to strike up a conversation with someone he would never see again. But at least it was something to do to take his mind off of the flight.

He might be a nervous passenger, but he was not completely rude, so with his eyes now fully opened, he turned to see an old man wearing a rumpled three-piece suit and bow tie. Completing the outfit, a Brooklyn Dodgers baseball cap atop a full mane of electrically charged white hair. Okay, the old guy got Gabe's attention, and despite his initial wariness, Gabe was happy for the diversion.

The old man began again, somewhat timidly, "My name is Phineas Foster."

He said it as if he assumed Gabe knew who he was.

Gabe introduced himself in turn, "I'm Gabriel Marx. Most people call me Gabe."

Gabe waited for the old man's next statement. But instead the old man shifted back around in his seat, lowered his cap over his eyes, and instantly started to snore, and loudly, very loudly, in neatly orchestrated phrases.

"Wait a minute here, someone actually gets my attention, and now I've lost his," Gabe heard himself saying louder than he realized.

Phineas Foster, that was a pretty weird name, Gabe thought, *but why did it sound so familiar?* He reached under his seat into his backpack, pulled out his iPad, and quickly turned it on. He tapped the keys, hopeful that his spelling might come close enough. "F-I-N-E-U-S F-A-W-S-T-E-R". Nothing! Another attempt, *maybe PH instead of F?* One of the few spelling rules he actually remembered.

And there it was, Phineas Jeremiah Foster, born 1915. Way too much to read, but enough highlighted simple words and photos for Gabe to get the information he needed. Phineas Jeremiah Foster, rumored to be the oldest living inventor in the world, credited with such notable gadgets as the instant multiple choice right answer retriever, the reading absorption device, the think out loud paragraph and essay writer, and the automatic homework correction pen. These were just a few of the crafty tools said to have made P.J. Foster a hero to schoolchildren around the globe. Well perhaps a hero to kids, but certainly not to the school districts which had long since banned Foster's inventions as nothing more than sophisticated cheating devices. At least that's how the stories went.

Now Gabe remembered. He had heard about the old guy, or at least he heard the rumors about him. The myths about Foster were legendary among middle schoolers, but no one had heard anything about him for the longest time. If P. J. Foster was real after all, what was he doing flying coach to New York? The last reports about Foster said he had vanished about thirty or so years ago. Some people even thought he was dead. Others were convinced that he never existed at all.

Well the famous and reclusive Professor Foster, or at least someone claiming to be Foster, was clearly alive, although possibly not so well. What's more, he managed to do the one thing Gabe could never do on a plane, sleep. And sleep he did for the next five hours, stirring only briefly to change positions in his seat. Any hope Gabe had of finding out if this guy was the real deal and what he was doing on this plane heading for New York was soon dashed upon arrival when the flight attendant swept up the aisle with a wheelchair to whisk him into the terminal before Gabe could ask him a single question.

Gabe tried to grab his carry-on bag from the crowded overhead compartment. By the time he wrenched it free of the shopping bags piled on top of it, any thought he had of chasing down the wheelchair was gone. As he pulled his bag free, he noticed a small spiral notebook, the kind Gabe never remembered to use for his homework assignments, in the seat pocket in front of where the old man had been sitting. Maybe if he could break though the line of passengers in front of him, there was a chance Gabe could catch the old guy at baggage claim and at least return the notebook or maybe even get his autograph. Proof positive that P.J. Foster really did exist and was still alive.

Gabe moved as fast as he could. Up and down escalators, he dodged passengers going to and from their gates. As he reached baggage claim, he spotted the flight attendant who had taken the professor off the plane. She was heading back in his direction. He cleared his throat and surprised by his own daring stopped her briefly to ask, "Where did you take that old guy? Did anyone meet him at baggage claim?"

"Nope, just put him in a cab. Do you know him or something?" replied the young woman. Gabe shook his head and just as he was about to tell her about the notebook, he stopped himself.

"Do you know where the taxi was headed?" Gabe asked instead.

She thought for a moment and answered, "He gave me a business card to hand the driver. I think it said something like Kingston or Kingman, no Kingsley, yeah that's it, Kingsley Institute."

With that the flight attendant rushed off back toward the gate and Gabe stood there bewildered. If Professor Foster was the real deal, why had he suddenly surfaced and what was he doing heading for the Kingsley Institute in New York? There was something about the Kingsley Institute that sounded familiar to Gabe, but he didn't know what. And then the light bulb went on. "The Kingsley Institute is run by that mind control geek my dad met last summer," Gabe suddenly blurted out.

Philip Kingsley was sort of an acquaintance of Gabe's father, Martin. Gabe had met him briefly last summer when his dad took him into the city for a day so he could attend some lawyers' conference, where Dr. Kingsley was presenting a paper on his research findings.

But even a brief meeting before Gabe went off for the day to visit his cousin who lived in Manhattan was enough for Philip Kingsley to make an impression on Gabe. He was about as wide as he was tall, a short rotund fellow with an annoyed stare firmly glued to his face, as if he were doing you a favor just speaking to you. He grunted more than he spoke, and whatever he said, he said as if he and only he knew anything about the subject.

What could Professor Phineas Jeremiah Foster have to do with the Kingsley Institute, let alone Dr. Philip Kingsley? Gabe hoped that the notebook might give him some answers. He wasn't quite sure that he would tell his dad about it, at least not right away. Gabe knew he would have to time this very carefully if he wanted to track down the old guy without arousing his father's curiosity too soon. No doubt, this would require endless promises of getting his summer reading done, and at least appearing not to stick his nose where it didn't belong. Well, some things might just be worth the sacrifice!

Chapter Two

Dad

Martin Marx was a name that Gabe's father, the esteemed New York attorney, learned to have a sense of humor about. Although he was teased endlessly, he was not related to Groucho, Harpo, or Karl for that matter. Gabe's great grandfather had simply shortened the actual family name from Marxekovicz when he arrived in the United States from Russia in 1920. Nevertheless, Gabe's dad endured many jokes about his name growing up in Brooklyn during the sixties.

He managed to survive the taunts of his street buddies and high school basketball teammates, eventually completing college and law school and moving to Los Angeles to take a job with a top law firm. He had established quite a reputation as a defense attorney in LA before moving back east after the divorce from Gabe's mom to start his own law firm.

Now he sat on his deck overlooking the water in Sag Harbor taking phone calls and answering emails as he waited for his only son, Gabe, to pull up in the driveway. It was tough on Gabe having a part-time dad, but that had been the arrangement for the past two years and both father and son had learned to make the best of it. Gabe knew his father thought he was a good kid. He also knew he could be a handful. There was always the struggle about his schoolwork, which Gabe knew his father couldn't quite understand. His dad had always been a straight-A student without having to make much of an effort. The school thing just did not come easily for Gabe.

As early as first grade, teachers complained that he was distractible, wasn't catching on to reading, couldn't sit still and so on. "He really is a bright young man, if he would only apply himself," was the refrain Gabe's parents heard at each parent-teacher meeting. Then there were the therapists and tutors, the frustration and resistance, and endless pep talks. There had been progress, but fundamentally Gabe knew the way his dad saw it, he always looked for the easy way out and saw the whole school thing as an unnecessary evil of childhood.

Martin glanced at his watch and rushed his secretary off the phone. He did his best to complete all of his business transactions before Gabe's arrival. After all, they hadn't seen each other since April when Gabe made his last visit east.

There were phone calls at least twice a week in between, but those were more like newscasts or press conferences, with formal question and answer exchanges. Lots of sound bites, but little substance, and even less of a connection between father and son. Gabe realized his dad couldn't help himself, always turning the conversation into something about school, something about grades. He was never able to take the discussion to another level where he might actually give himself a chance to know his son.

They both looked forward to the visits. They genuinely enjoyed each other's company, shared a love of sports, old black and white detective movies, and long walks on the beach. They were more alike than either of them cared to admit, but it always took time to go through a warming up phase, a transition from acting like father and son to being father and son.

"They should have arrived by now," Gabe's dad mumbled to himself. He glanced at his watch and suspected that the driver had probably gotten caught up in traffic on the Long Island Expressway. After all, this was the July fourth weekend and everyone was heading out to the beaches for the holiday. Just as he picked up his cell phone to check with the driver, the phone signaled an incoming text message. *Need you back in the city ASAP. Major problems with the Harvey trial. Jeff.* Jeffrey Rogers was Gabe's dad's law firm partner and rarely took time off to breathe, let alone for a holiday weekend. He must have forgotten that Martin was expecting Gabe, which was typical for the workaholic lawyer who didn't seem to have a life outside of the office.

Gabe's dad couldn't imagine what the big deal was with the Harvey trial. Leonard Harvey was your typical shady businessman who had gotten caught with his hand in someone else's pocket. Something to do with fraud or forging bank records to the tune of a few hundred million dollars. Martin couldn't understand what the big deal could be that required him to drop everything and battle holiday traffic to get back to Manhattan. Jeff was about the most competent lawyer around. If anyone could get Harvey off without jail time, it was Jeff. He certainly didn't need his help with this. And besides, the court was in recess until next Tuesday.

As he was about to text Jeff back, the house phone rang. Martin expected the housekeeper to answer it until he realized she had left early for the weekend. He managed to grab it on the fourth ring, banging his shin on the coffee table as he raced past the living room to the desk in his study.

"Marty, you've got to get back here. Harvey's gone," Jeff whispered.

"What do ya mean gone?" Martin answered.

"I mean gone as in dead," Jeff said.

"How?" Martin asked.

"Well at first it seemed like a heart attack, but since he died alone in his apartment, the coroner insisted on an autopsy. They found traces of a cardio toxic substance in his blood, which in large amounts causes heart failure. The bottom line, Marty, is that he was murdered," Jeff explained.

Gabe's dad could hardly believe what he was hearing. The law firm of Marx and Rogers didn't do murder. Embezzlement, fraud, forgery, and other white collar crime, but nothing violent, and certainly not murder. Martin couldn't imagine what one of their clients was into that would have lead to his violent death. And why now, when he hadn't seen his son for three months?

As Martin hung up the phone, he heard the crunch of gravel as the car pulled into the driveway. Gabe had finally arrived and Martin had to ask the driver to turn right around and get him back to the city so he could calm Jeff down. He had no idea how he was going to explain this to Gabe. He needed to be a responsible dad for the next few weeks, not some big shot attorney who put his son on hold and went rushing off so he could make headlines, or in this case, avoid making headlines. He loved Jeff like a brother, and he certainly was devoted to his law practice, but he had to keep his priorities straight for once. No, he'd call Jeff back and tell him he just had to handle this one on his own.

Chapter Three

Dad's Dilemma

The ride out to eastern Long Island seemed never ending. There was the usual tangle of taxicabs outside of the airport terminal, no doubt made worse by the winding stream of travelers heading to or from the city for the holiday weekend. Then there was the parade of trucks and SUV's hogging the road so the run of the mill passenger cars had to struggle to take their rightful place on the ramp to the Long Island Expressway. Gabe was impressed with the idea that he was being picked up by his father's driver, but a bit disappointed to discover that the limousine he had fantasized about was a pretty ordinary Volvo sedan.

Once out of the airport and on the highway, the driver made pretty good time. Things started to slow down as the Hamptons holiday traffic caught up with them when they exited the expressway. They followed the stop and go, bumper-to-bumper crowds to the various beach communities. It seemed like it was taking forever. Gabe had declined the driver's offer to sit up front with him, and instead chose the back seat where he thought he would have a little more privacy. He needed some time to get a closer look at the old man's notebook and think through this whole P.J. Foster incident without a lot of unnecessary small talk with the driver.

The first several pages of the notebook contained a string of formulas and other scientific notations, which made no sense to Gabe. However, he was now convinced about two things. Phineas Foster was real and indeed he had been sitting next to him on the plane.

"Hey there, young Master Marx, what are you reading back there?" the driver interrupted.

"Nothing," Gabe said.

He nervously tucked the notebook into his backpack before he was confronted with any more questions.

Although patience was never Gabe's strong suit he would have to wait until he was safely in his room at his dad's to check out the rest of the notebook.

What's more, Gabe was exhausted. He might not have been able to fall asleep on the plane, but back on terra firma, he did just that, fell asleep. He never heard the young driver Pete McDonough ask him if he was hungry or needed a bathroom.

That's what woke him up. He had to go so badly because in his excitement about the old man, and helping Pete grab his suitcase off the luggage carousel, he got into the car without stopping to heed his mother's famous refrain.

"Try to go before we leave because once we get into the car there won't be any decent place to stop for a bathroom."

That was the key, any decent place. Gabe wouldn't just pee anywhere, certainly not in any roadside gas station toilet, and by no means, absolutely positively not in the bushes along the highway.

"Well I see you're back among the living," Pete declared.

Gabe stretched his arms and wiggled about in his seat hoping he could hold out until they reached his dad's house.

"How much longer until we get there?" Gabe asked. He hoped for the answer he wanted to hear.

"Actually, you missed the worst of it. The traffic was pretty bad. Your dad tried to call on the cell phone, but I couldn't hear him on the other end. I'd say about another ten minutes or so depending upon whether we get stuck at the traffic light." Gabe took a deep breath, did another wiggle and uncrossed and crossed his legs, moving awkwardly from one position to another.

Gabe unfastened his seatbelt as the car pulled into the driveway. As soon as the engine stopped, the door flew open, and he raced past his father through the garage into the small guest bathroom off of the kitchen. His dad stood there, arms outstretched to welcome his son when he saw the flash of the blue Mets jersey whisk by him. Pete explained Gabe's desperate need for a toilet and then helped Martin unload the duffel from the trunk of the sedan.

By the time the two men carried Gabe's bags upstairs, he emerged from the downstairs bathroom with a look of relief on his face. His dad told him to help himself to a snack from the refrigerator.

No sooner were the words out of his mouth, "Don't overdo it or you'll ruin your appetite," that Gabe realized his dad was doing it again, starting off his visit with a warning.

His dad couldn't quite seem to avoid it. Gabe knew his father wanted him to feel at home, so why did he have to anticipate his lack of self-control, always punctuating their visits by setting limits?

Gabe was used to the warnings and admonishments. He was either doing too much of something or not enough of something else pretty much most of the time. This was the part of his dad that he dreaded, but it was all part of the package deal and it wasn't made any easier by the fact that they didn't get to see each other very often. But he was determined not to let it get to him this time, particularly now when he needed to get to the bottom of this Phineas Foster business.

Martin appeared in the kitchen, following Pete down the stairs to the first floor of the house. Cell phone in hand, he was talking to Jeff Rogers at the office, obviously trying to convince him about something. He asked Pete not to leave just yet.

"No problem, Mr. M. I've got no place special I need to get to. In fact, I have no plans for dinner just in case anyone is curious."

Gabe wasn't too keen about having Pete join him and his dad on their first evening together. But then again, maybe it would take the edge off. Pete seemed like a cool enough guy.

"Okay, okay," Gabe overheard his dad on the phone.

"But not tonight. Gabe just got here. Tomorrow morning, you'll just have to hold them off until tomorrow morning. You're a Harvard graduate; you'll think of something."

His dad was trying to handle some sort of client problem. He did his best, but there was no convincing Jeff. He wanted his law partner back in the city. There were police crawling all over their office with subpoenas for confidential files, and reporters were calling with all kinds of questions.

His dad turned off the cell phone and placed it in his shirt pocket. He tried to find the words to explain why he would have to interrupt his first visit with his son in three months. Gabe looked up from his bowl of ice cream topped with rice crispies and marshmallows. He tried not to seem too excited about the prospect of returning to the city with his father.

"What's up, Dad? Sounds like you have to head back to the city tomorrow."

His father explained there was a small problem with a client, without revealing too many details. He suggested that Gabe could hang out at the house with Pete for the day and he would be back by early evening, hopefully in time for dinner.

"How are you going to get to Manhattan if Pete hangs out here with me?" Gabe asked.

Of course he had another motive, but tried not to be too obvious, at least not just yet.

"Pete and I will need a car to get around out here, Dad, so you can't drive," Gabe continued. He actually made a pretty good lawyer-like case, much to his own surprise.

"Well, I don't want to ruin the first full day of your vacation by dragging you back to the city with me," Martin answered in a genuinely concerned fatherly way.

"I could take the bus or the train. Problem is the holiday schedule is so unpredictable."

Gabe was careful not to answer too quickly for fear of arousing his father's suspicions about his sudden eagerness to leave the beach and head into the blistering heat of the city in July.

"Well, it's just one day, Dad, and I actually met someone on the plane I would like to check on while you're busy with Jeff and your clients at the office."

His dad was not suspicious yet, but he was certainly curious about Gabe's new acquaintance. As Martin was about to question Gabe further, the cell phone rang again with an urgency that Martin knew could not be good news.

Jeff was on the other end again, pleading with Martin to turn on the TV immediately.

"Not now, Jeff. Gabe just got here. What's so important?"

"What's so important? They have a suspect in the murder of Leonard Harvey," Jeff replied anxiously, "The police have issued a warrant for the arrest of Professor Phineas Jeremiah Foster!"

Chapter Four

Suspicion of Murder

Gabe stared at the TV in disbelief. He had just been sitting next to this old guy on the plane a few hours ago, and now he was listening to a news reporter describe him as a murder suspect. Martin slid over on the couch, making room for Gabe and Pete in front of the huge screen in the den. He held the cell phone in one hand and the remote in the other, trying to listen to Jeff and channel surf at the same time to get the latest update on the arrest.

There it was, unmistakably reported on CNN for the entire world to hear.

"Following the discovery of the body of Leonard Harvey, at first thought to have died from natural causes, the Manhattan assistant district attorney, Penelope Cooper, has just issued an arrest warrant for Phineas Jeremiah Foster on suspicion of murder."

Suddenly dozens of photos flashed on the screen-- P.J. Foster as a young inventor, P.J. Foster in his laboratory surrounded by school children, P.J. Foster at the White House with scientists and dignitaries from around the world. All archived photos and footage from years ago, and then nothing at all about Foster for the past thirty years, not since the scandal over his controversial inventions.

And then the question every reporter and police officer had, "Where had Foster been for the last thirty years and where was P.J. Foster now?" A nationwide search was underway, but for the moment at least, his whereabouts were unknown.

What was the possible connection between the once esteemed and now disgraced Professor Foster and the infamous and rather shady Leonard Harvey? Penelope Cooper was about to give a press conference, which might shed some light on the whole matter. There she was, all five feet, one inch of her, with so many microphones crowding her face it was almost impossible to detect a person standing behind the podium in front of City Hall. This was a pretty high profile case with Harvey accused of embezzling well over one hundred million dollars from the pension fund of city workers.

Gabe sat next to his dad awaiting the start of the assistant district attorney's opening statement. He observed the clearly agonized expression on his father's face. "I never wanted to take the Harvey case. This was not the kind of publicity we needed or wanted. This was workaholic, ambitious Jeff's idea," Martin recalled.

"'This will be good for us, Marty. This is just the kind of case we need to get us on the map'," Martin said, imitating the refrain he heard over and over again from his law partner. "Sure this case will get the law firm of Marx and Rogers on the map... the map to Alcatraz," Gabe's dad muttered sarcastically.

By the time the press conference was over, Penelope Cooper had explained that Professor Phineas Foster was the prime suspect in the murder of Leonard Harvey. He had motive, personally having been cheated out of hundreds of thousands of dollars by Mr. Harvey. He had means, having access to drugs as part of his most recent scientific work. He had opportunity, having met with Mr. Harvey two days earlier in an undisclosed location outside of Los Angeles.

It was at that meeting that it was suspected that the alleged murderer switched Harvey's heart medication with the lethal dose of Doxepin, a known cardio-toxic drug. Penelope Cooper also confirmed that Professor Foster was indeed missing, and hadn't been seen since yesterday when he asked his housekeeper to pack a bag for him for a trip he would be taking the next day.

If Gabe's dad appeared to be in agony over these developments, Gabe was actually in ecstasy. Puzzled, perhaps, but overwhelmingly joyous at how not boring this visit was turning out to be and how preoccupied his father was, and thus much less likely to be on his case about summer homework.

Of course, Gabe had never gotten to tell his father the identity of the acquaintance that he made on the plane or that he was in possession of the notebook the professor left behind. Given the circumstances, that was probably just as well. In fact, that whole line of questioning had come to an end with Jeff's phone call, the flood of TV coverage about the embezzlement, murder, and the disappearance of the one and only suspect.

There was of course, one other little tidbit of information, a minor matter that Gabe would have to decide what to do with sooner or later. He was indeed the last person to have seen or spoken to P.J. Foster, unless the flight attendant who escorted him to the cab, or the cab driver, counted.

For the time being, Gabe would try to direct his father's attention back to the idea of heading into the city. At least that would give him an opportunity to check out the Kingsley Institute, the likely location of the most wanted murder suspect in New York City.

Gabe's dad turned off the TV, got up from the couch, and starting pacing around the den as if he were in a fog. It was nearly nine o'clock and none of them had eaten dinner. "Gee, Gabe, I am so sorry about how this evening has turned out," he said apologetically. "Pete, could you go into town and pick up some pizzas for us. When you get back, we'll figure this all out."

"Sure thing, Mr. M.," Pete replied, "I'll be back in a jiffy. How's pepperoni, mushrooms, and extra cheese?" he asked as he was halfway out the door. Gabe looked at his dad, and they both nodded their heads simult-aneously, approving of the menu.

"Gabe, you must be exhausted as well as starved," his dad said. Gabe understood that his dad was trying to stay focused on his fatherly duties and more importantly, not incur Gabe's mom's wrath. Both Gabe and he knew she would call any minute now to find out how Gabe is doing, whether he's eaten, and if he did any reading before bed tonight.

Gabe was about as wide-awake as he could be, and bursting with his secret about his airplane encounter with a famous inventor and now notorious murderer.

"I'm great, Dad. Actually, I'm a little worried about you," Gabe responded with genuine concern. Through-out the course of the evening, he had seen his father's complexion go from suntanned and robust to gray and dismal.

Gabe's dad then took a few minutes to explain his and Jeff's connection to this whole mess.

"Leonard Harvey was due to go on trial in a few weeks and Jeff and I were representing him. We were his defense attorneys in this whole fiasco," Martin confessed to his son.

"I will have to head back to the city tomorrow. The police want to talk to Jeff and me. They're already all over our records like flies on honey. I can't expect Jeff to handle this much longer on his own."

With that, Gabe saw his opening, "Dad, let me come with you. Maybe I can help."

There was something more to this that Gabe couldn't quite put his finger on. Whatever he lacked in book smarts, he made up for in intuition. And at this moment, his instincts were kicking in big time. He couldn't get the thought out of his head. Whether it made sense or not, whether the professor was or was not a murderer, the old man needed his help.

"Gabe, your mother would kill me if I let you get involved in this. This is your vacation and I'm supposed to handle your visit like a responsible adult. I'll see if the housekeeper Lilly can stay with you for a day or two until I can get this all straightened out."

"Dad, I'm already involved in this," Gabe interjected with some hesitation, "The person I met on the plane, the one I mentioned before, well, he wasn't a kid. Actually, he was a pretty old guy."

"Gabe, why do you want to make a trip back into the city to check on some old guy?" his dad asked.

Gabe realized that his father couldn't quite understand where this apparent confession was coming from. And then Gabe watched the gray dismal look on his father's face from a few minutes earlier turn to a greenish nausea as he realized where Gabe was going with this explanation.

"No," Martin uttered with a hushed sense of terror in his voice.

"Yes," Gabe answered. "I was probably the last person to speak with Professor Foster just before he got off the plane at JFK," he reported to his father. *And I'm probably the only one who knows where he was going when he left the airport,* he thought to himself, but certainly was not ready to reveal to his dad.

Chapter Five

Half a Confession Is Better Than None

"Hey, I'm back," Pete announced. He tumbled into the kitchen trying to balance the pizza boxes and bottles of soda with one hand as he closed the door to the garage with the other.

"Whoa, who died? Uh oh, on second thought that was probably a pretty dumb thing to say under the circumstances."

But the look on Martin's face was downright scary, "What's up, Mr. M.? You don't look so good."

Pete's arrival back at the house startled Martin as he tried to concentrate on what Gabe was telling him. It was obvious to Gabe that his father didn't want to continue the conversation in front of Pete.

Gabe saw the shock on his father's face as he revealed who his seatmate was on the flight from Los Angeles. He also knew that as a lawyer, his dad would have to pass along this information to the assistant district attorney and the police, even though it would mean involving his son. But Gabe realized that what probably made his father shudder most was how his mom would react to what was happening in the less than twenty-four hours that he had been in New York, the city she called the Bad Apple. This was, of course, a sarcastic reference to the TV ads inviting tourists from everywhere to the Big Apple. Since the divorce and Gabe's dad's decision to relocate to New York City, Gabe's mom, Eleanor, better known as Elly, pretty much detested the Bad Apple.

"It's nothing," Martin assured Pete, "It's probably something I ate for lunch. You guys go ahead and eat the pizza. I'm not really that hungry and I've got some phone calls to make to get ready to head back into the city tomorrow."

Gabe knew any plan to return to the city would have to include him now, even if only briefly, to tell the assistant district attorney and the police whatever he knew. He was fully aware he had not confessed everything. He told his dad about the brief conversation, if you could call it that, with P.J. Foster on the plane. He told him about trying to follow him off the plane and running into the flight attendant who had put the old man in a cab at JFK. He did leave out two other little pieces of information, the part about the Kingsley Institute, and, of course, the notebook.

When his dad asked Gabe if he knew where Professor Foster was going, he just shook his head. He hated lying to his dad, but he preferred to think of this as an omission, not a lie. He had overheard enough of his father's lawyer discussions to conclude that he was withholding information rather than actually lying, a technicality perhaps, but one that relieved his guilt a little bit, at least for the moment.

As Gabe's dad walked upstairs to his study, the house phone rang with that sense of urgency again. He checked the caller I.D. but didn't recognize the number.

The call was coming from the city as the display indicated a 212 area code, but the rest of the number was unfamiliar.

"Martin, hi, it's Penny, Penelope Cooper," the voice on the other end announced. This phone call had to come sooner or later, given the law firm of Marx and Rogers' connection to the murder victim.

"I didn't want to have to deal with this conversation tonight," Martin mumbled to himself.

"Jeff Rogers gave me your phone number out there. Sorry to disturb you over the holiday, but things are developing very quickly," she explained.

Gabe listened in on the conversation as best he could. He observed his father shake his head in agreement as he made arrangements with Penny Cooper for the meeting the next morning.

When he got off the phone, his dad explained that he first met Penelope Cooper at Pacific Law School outside of Los Angeles, when she was still a student.

"She was quite a little dynamo, even back then, so it's no surprise that she was asked to handle a high profile case like the Harvey murder," he said.

"Should I take the fifth?" Gabe asked, once again trying to display his lawyer like skill.

"Very funny, Gabe. No, just tell her the truth," his dad advised, still unaware that he had not gotten the full story.

Gabe's dad made arrangements to pick Jeff up at his Upper East Side apartment and to drive downtown to meet with Cooper the next morning. He had not yet told Jeff about Gabe and Foster. That could wait until the ride downtown. He sent Pete home, at least for a few hours, telling him to pick him and Gabe up at six in the morning.

"There probably won't be much traffic heading into the city on a Saturday because of the holiday weekend, but let's not take any chances. Time to hit the sack, Gabe."

"No problem, Dad," Gabe responded.

He was anxious to get to his room and have a few private moments to check out the notebook he had hidden away earlier. It might contain information that would help him get to the bottom of this.

The next phone call, not unexpected at all, was Elly Marshall, alias Marx. She had gone back to using her maiden name after the divorce. An artist living in Venice Beach, California, a single mom totally devoted to her son, she never let Gabe's dad forget how difficult it was to raise a child alone. She had pretty much cornered the market on guilt. Actually, if you could get a college degree in guilt, Gabe's mom had earned her Ph.D. hands down.

"Is everything all right? I've been trying to call for hours. Don't you have call waiting? Did you have the phone off the hook? Is Gabe okay?" Elly asked.

She barely stopped to take a breath between questions.

Gabe's dad held the phone several inches from his ear waiting for the interrogation to stop. When she came up for air, he reassured her that everything was fine and then made up some excuse about a problem he was having with the phone line.

Martin caught up with Gabe on the staircase and signaled him to pick up the extension and speak to his mom. He put his finger to his lips and mouthed his plea that Gabe not mention any of this to his mother over the phone. Gabe was more than happy to go along with his dad's request. He loved knowing that they had this secret between them and that no one had even bothered to check on whether he did any reading on the plane, or if he had worked out his daily summer homework schedule.

Well that didn't last too long. As soon as Elly was convinced that all was well in Sag Harbor, she reminded Gabe about the work his tutor asked him to complete during vacation, and of course his promise to email his daily reading log to her.

"Got it, Mom. Yes, I will. Love you, Mom. Speak to you in a few days," Gabe replied.

He did his best not to seem to rush her off the phone. He knew that she had a sixth sense where he was concerned, and didn't want to do anything that would make her suspicious.

His dad stood by, listening to the brief conversation and breathed a momentary sigh of relief.

"Okay Gabe, we got a little off track tonight, but once this is all straightened out tomorrow, we'll get back onto a schedule."

Gabe realized that his dad was doing all he could to convince himself that he had the situation under control.

"Don't worry Dad, I don't really know that much. I just flew to New York with the old guy. He didn't tell me anything that would make me an accessory to the murder or anything like that." Gabe was starting to get pretty good at this legal talk.

And indeed, Gabe was not lying this time either, because P.J. Foster had not told him anything. Whatever he knew about the professor's whereabouts came from questioning the flight attendant who put the old man in a cab. For the moment, all he could think about was getting another look at the notebook, now hidden securely in the back pocket of his jeans, driving into the city the next day and figuring out how he could lose his dad long enough to check out the Kingsley Institute.

Chapter Six

The Whole Truth and Nothing but the Truth

The drive into Manhattan was uneventful. As Gabe's dad predicted, there was very little traffic as Pete merged onto the expressway. Fully awake this time, Gabe engaged in his usual how to make the time pass in the car activity, guessing how many out of state license plates he would see, and which car would have traveled the longest distance to reach New York. Forty-three sightings and eight states later, most of them New Jersey and Connecticut, Gabe finally spotted one he had never seen before, North Dakota. He looked up just as the car approached the exit for the 59th Street Bridge, the last exit in Queens before crossing the East River into Manhattan.

As Gabe saw the billboards and vast geometry of Manhattan's impressive skyscrapers, he lost track of the license plates and focused once again on his mission to get to the bottom of Professor Foster's sudden reappearance and even more sudden disappearance. He had no idea how he would manage to conduct his own investigation under his father's watchful eye, but then again Gabe was never big on planning, or at least that was what his teachers always said.

"Gabriel, maybe you should think that problem through more carefully before you start," and, "Gabriel, you need to put an outline together before you try to write your essay."

Gabe simply could not see any point to doing more than he had to do to get things done. Why would anyone do extra things when they could just get started on the thing they needed to do in the first place? The whole business never made much sense to him in the past, but at this particular moment, he began to realize that planning might not be such a bad idea after all.

While Gabe debated the pros and cons of planning with himself, the only thing his dad could talk about on the drive into the city was his plan — his plan for what he would tell Jeff Rogers, his plan for the meeting with Penny Cooper, his plan for what to do with Gabe while they were in the city, and most importantly, his plan for what he would say to Gabe's mother to make certain that she didn't doubt his ability as a father.

Pete made a left turn off the bridge to First Avenue, and then drove up to East 66th Street to Jeff's apartment. Jeff had already made three phone calls and sent as many text messages to Martin during the drive to check the time of their arrival. As expected, he was waiting on the corner, bagel hanging out of his mouth, coffee cup carefully balanced in one hand while he held his briefcase and spoke on the phone with the other.

Jeff was surprised to see Gabe in the car, having expected that Martin would have left him back at the house with the housekeeper. Jumping into the back seat next to Gabe, he couldn't quite hide his discomfort with the almost teen. It was pretty clear to Gabe that Jeff was all work and didn't have any great fondness for preadolescent kids. Gabe knew Jeff wanted his dad's full attention with the Harvey matter, and didn't want him to be distracted trying to be the good father.

"Hey Gabe, how's school?" Jeff asked. He seemed about as interested in the answer as Gabe was in the question.

Martin joined in before Gabe could answer and informed Jeff about Gabe's trip to New York and his seatmate on the flight from Los Angeles. Jeff managed to hit all three of the cars' other passengers as the coffee cup flew out of his hand and the remaining bite of bagel was launched from his mouth as he almost choked.

"Take it easy Jeff. This was all just an amazing coincidence. Gabe doesn't know anything else," Martin reassured his partner as Jeff scrambled to clean himself off and regain his composure.

Gabe struggled with whether or not to reveal anything else at that moment. He wanted to tell his father what he knew, but not just yet, at least not until he could figure out why Professor Foster was headed to the Kingsley Institute.

"Hold on a minute, let me get this straight," Jeff said, having calmed down and retrieved most of his airborne breakfast. Gabe told Jeff the story, pretty much word for word as he had explained it to his dad the night before, again only omitting the very last bit of information about the flight attendant, the cab, the Kingsley Institute, and, of course the notebook.

Jeff was relieved for the moment, believing Gabe had no other knowledge of Phineas Foster. However, his anxiety subsided only temporarily as he remembered that the police detectives were all over his and Martin's office since last night, and they were heading for a meeting with the assistant district attorney.

"Jeff, we have nothing to hide," Martin said.

Once again he tried to reassure his partner, "If anything, Gabe will be able to confirm that Foster did arrive in New York yesterday, somewhere around the time that Harvey's body was discovered. Come to think of it, that does make it a little tougher for the assistant district attorney to pin this thing on Foster. How does a 100-year-old guy manage to arrive in New York, commit murder, and vanish in under an hour? No matter what, once the police know that Foster is in town, they're gonna focus on finding and questioning him. That should take the heat off of us and give us some time to figure out how to deal with our end of things," Martin continued. He did his best to appear confident that he had a handle on things.

"Sure Marty, and now that you've established an implausible timeline for the assistant district attorney, with your son as the suspect's only alibi for the murder of our client, that should really take the heat off of us," Jeff replied in his characteristically sarcastic way.

"Keep in mind that Cooper said it was suspected that Foster switched the drugs two days ago in LA. It's our dumb luck that Harvey croaked in New York. It's hard to know whose jurisdiction this murder rap will fall under when all is said and done. If we really get lucky, we'll have the LAPD and the NYPD to deal with before long," Jeff continued.

"Okay, this is getting rather messy," Gabe's dad mumbled under his breath, "But let's just take this one step at a time. We'll see what Penelope Cooper wants from us, and how Gabe's confirmation that Foster arrived in New York yesterday does or doesn't help her case," he said. Once again, he seemed to be trying to reassure himself more than anyone else at the moment.

Pete had been quiet during the drive downtown, winding his way through the typical Manhattan construction street closures to reach the City Hall area and the assistant district attorney's office. He listened intently, taking it all in, and not saying anything unless he was asked. And so far, on this trip the only question he was asked was how much longer until they arrived. He had his own questions about Gabe's strange encounter on the plane and for some reason, call it instinct, didn't quite believe that Gabe had told his dad the whole story.

"Okay, let us off here," Martin said, as they pulled up in front of the towering office building.

If this had been a weekday, the streets would be filled with people, but on the Saturday of this uncomfortably warm July fourth weekend, only a handful of jacketless city workers waited for the elevator to reach their floors. In fact, there was no secretary at the front desk of the suite of offices, and responding to the security guard's alert a few minutes earlier, Penelope Cooper herself greeted Martin, Jeff, and surprisingly Gabe as they entered.

"Thanks for coming in," she said. She looked puzzled when she saw Martin and Jeff accompanied by the boy. She knew Martin was divorced and guessed that he certainly could have a child about this boy's age. She just didn't understand why they would have brought him along. But then again, her own child, Alex, was keeping busy in her office since she too had to cut her holiday weekend short to deal with the Harvey murder, and couldn't arrange for a sitter without more notice.

After the brief introduction and Penelope's assumption that Martin couldn't make child care arrangements either on such short notice, she suggested that Gabe could join Alex in her office and play some computer games. Gabe was delighted at having an excuse to get away from his dad for a while, particularly if Alex turned out to be a good guy and there was a computer available in his mom's office to do some snooping.

Martin was relieved to know that Gabe might have someone to hang out with since this business was likely to take several hours.

"That's great," he said thankfully. This would give him and Jeff time to meet with the assistant district attorney alone first before bringing up the whole airplane encounter with Foster.

Gabe followed Penelope down the long corridor to her office, amazed at the seemingly mile high shelves of law books lining the walls. He knew that lawyers were really into reading, which is why he knew, much to his father's dismay, that he would never be a lawyer. He just couldn't get it; *there had to be better ways of learning things than reading*, he thought to himself.

Just then, Penelope pushed the door to her office open and called out, "Alex, there's someone I'd like you to meet."

Gabe could hardly see the young boy bent over the computer, which was partially concealed by a pile of his mother's law books. Alex barely looked up from behind the computer as Gabe followed Penelope into the office.

"Hey, earth to Alex," Penelope called out again, "Gabe, I'd like you to meet Alexandra Cooper, Alex for short," she exclaimed.

Oh great, Gabe thought to himself. He swallowed hard and realized he would now have to spend several hours trying to figure out what to talk to a girl about. He almost wished he had brought a book along to read.

Chapter Seven

Digging Up the Facts

Alex, completely engrossed by the computer screen, looked up rather startled to see her mother and what's his name standing in the doorway of the office.

"What are you up to, Alex?" Penelope inquired, "I want you to meet my colleague's son, Gabe. I'm going to be meeting with his dad for a while. Do you think you guys could keep each other occupied for about an hour or so?" she continued.

She didn't want to give Alex a chance to object, knowing that she was generally a loner and not big on sharing with other kids. Alex could be pretty possessive of her things and didn't seem to have much patience for children her own age, let alone boys.

"We'll be right down the hall in the conference room if you need us." Penelope's voice trailed off as she turned her back without giving Alex a chance to protest.

Now what? thought Gabe, feeling completely uncomfortable and frustrated. He had work to do and no time to spare making small talk with some girl. He needed to get to that computer and find out whatever he could about P.J. Foster and the Kingsley Institute. He needed time to see if he could make any sense out of the formulas scribbled in the notebook he had concealed in his backpack.

Gabe knew enough not to jump in and make his request immediately. He could be charming if he wanted to be. In fact, he was pretty good at covering up his awkwardness with guys, but girls were a whole other ball game.

"Hey Alex, what are you working on?" Gabe asked politely enough.

"Nothing that would interest you." Alex replied. She was anxious to put an end to that line of questioning.

"Okay, but how do you know that for sure?" Gabe tried again.

"Because kids your age are never interested in archaeology," Alex said impatiently.

"Well you have a point there since I don't even know what it is," Gabe answered, somewhat embarrassed. School was not his thing and if this was a subject he should have been paying attention to, he hadn't even heard of it.

Alex giggled at Gabe's confession, not laughing at him as much as finding his honesty amusing and unusual. Just about every other kid she knew found her obsession with archaeology boring. Kids at Emory Middle School usually poked fun at her and told her 'to get a life.' They nicknamed her 'The Excavator' and teased her about getting her head out of the sand whenever she seemed to be in a daze, which was pretty often. She was usually preoccupied with some archaeological dig she had heard or read about in the paper, hoping that one day she would get the chance to travel to an exotic location and unearth some yet undiscovered ancient culture herself.

Gabe needed to get over to that computer one way or another and if finding out about arche-whatever-ology would do the trick, it was worth it.

"Well, I don't have a clue what you're talking about, but I'm willing to find out if you don't mind showing me," Gabe said. He was half thinking this might be fun and the other half trying to stay focused on the Foster matter.

Alex knew that giving Gabe a long explanation about archaeology would probably just bore him to death, so she logged onto a website with some really cool photos of digs in the desert and people uncovering parts of buildings and objects that were thousands of years old. Photos worked just fine for Gabe as long as Alex kept talking. He was just grateful that she didn't give him anything too complicated to read. He was happy to confess not knowing about archaeology, but there was no way he was letting on to Alex about his reading, not now and not ever if there was any way he could avoid it.

Gabe, who could hardly ever sit still long enough to listen to much of an explanation of anything, found himself really getting into this. Alex made it pretty interesting, more like an ancient whodunit than something you would learn in school.

He almost forgot why he was trying to get onto the computer in the first place when a slide appeared on the screen with the caption 'Tragic death of Dr. Jonas Foster ruled accidental, read more...' Gabe was certain that seeing the name Foster was just a strange coincidence, and he definitely didn't want to read more... but he asked Alex to click on the link just out of curiosity. Up popped a series of paragraphs and more photos of Dr. Jonas Foster.

Excusing himself from reading because he didn't have his glasses and was having trouble seeing the screen, Gabe asked Alex to fill him in on the story.

"Oh, this Dr. Foster was working on a dig in Egypt," Alex explained, "He was found dead at the site after going off by himself one morning. It wouldn't have been such a big deal, but he was the grandson of that old famous inventor guy P.J. Foster."

"How did he die?" Gabe asked. He tried to stay calm, but nearly jumped out of his skin.

"His death was ruled an accident. Well actually, what it says here is that it was believed that he had wandered into an area of the dig that hadn't yet been excavated. He slipped when he got his foot caught in a crevice in the rocks. He probably died of heat exposure and dehydration since it was several days until he was found."

"Is that all it says? Does it say anything else about him and his grandfather or when this happened?" Gabe spoke with surprising curiosity for someone who knew nothing about archaeology a few minutes earlier.

"Wait, there is something else," Alex went on, "They did an autopsy and suspect that the actual cause of death may have been a heart attack. Further toxicology reports are expected to confirm the cause of death and determine whether his fall triggered the heart attack or the heart attack triggered his fall."

"When did this happen?" Gabe persisted.

"It says that Dr. Foster was part of an expedition consisting of various scientific experts. The group had worked at various sites in Israel, Jordan, and Egypt, and was due to report back when the accident occurred. The expedition was discontinued and Dr. Jonas Foster's body was flown back to Los Angeles two weeks ago."

"Anything else, Alex? Anything at all?" Gabe said. He hoped for some connection to the old man.

"Nothing much," Alex said, "Just something about how the expedition was funded. Gee, that's funny," Alex said looking puzzled, "These kinds of digs are usually funded by the governments of the countries involved or university grants. This one was funded by a group of private investors including the scientist Dr. Philip Kingsley and businessman Leonard Harvey."

Gabe almost fell out of his chair, and was having serious difficulty staying calm with this latest revelation.

"Gabe, you look like you just saw a ghost," Alex said.

She looked at her recent archaeology convert trying to figure out exactly what was going on.

"Alex, do you have any idea what your mom and my dad are meeting about along with that nut case of an associate my father brought with him?" Gabe asked.

He wondered if Alex ever pulled herself away from the computer long enough to realize what was happening in the rest of the world.

Gabe completed the picture for Alex, including the murder of his dad's client, Leonard Harvey, the suspect who apparently had disappeared, and one more thing, the fact that he, Gabriel Marx, was probably the last person to see P.J. Foster, unless you counted the flight attendant or cab driver.

Chapter Eight

Now You See Me, Now You Don't

Gabe's dad looked at Jeff with a sigh of relief as the meeting with the assistant district attorney began to wind down. Penelope Cooper's questions were polite, but very thorough and very intense. A preliminary search of their office records did indicate that P.J. Foster had turned over a great deal of money to Harvey for investment purposes. In fact, there were dozens of files connecting Leonard Harvey to clients whose money he was accused of embezzling. It was puzzling as to why P.J. Foster was the only murder suspect given all the enemies Harvey had made during the past year. But the district attorney's office was certainly not going to reveal anything else about their evidence to Martin or Jeff, not in the middle of a high profile murder investigation like this.

Penelope offered the usual cautionary warning, "Keep in mind that so far we have only conducted a preliminary examination of your files. Given what we've found so far, your firm does not seem to be involved in any wrongdoing. We will be taking a closer look over the next days and weeks, and ask that you remain available for further questioning."

As Penelope shifted in her seat and began to get up, Gabe's dad volunteered the one piece of information he would have done anything to avoid having to reveal.

"There is something else, Penny, having nothing to do with our representation of Mr. Harvey," Martin said in a hesitant half whisper.

"What is it?" Penelope asked curiously.

Martin responded, providing whatever information he had about Gabe's bizarrely coincidental and brief encounter with P.J. Foster on the LA to New York flight the day before. Jeff paced back and forth nervously as Penelope sat back down in her chair with a look of disbelief on her face. Martin did everything he could to make light of his son's strange meeting at thirty-five thousand feet.

"Marty, are you telling me that Gabe can verify the professor's arrival in New York, and that he may have been one of the last people to see P.J. Foster before he disappeared yesterday?" Penelope said aloud. She wanted to make certain she had not mistaken what she had just heard.

"Seems that's right," Martin confirmed.

"You know I will have to talk to him, and I assume since you're telling me this, that I have your permission to question him further," she continued.

Martin nodded his head in agreement and followed Penelope down the corridor to her office where they left Gabe and Alex to occupy each other an hour earlier.

Jeff trailed behind, bringing up the rear of the procession through the floor to ceiling book-shelved hallway. Just before they reached the doorway to Penelope's office, Martin stepped in front of the assistant district attorney to reassure himself as well as her that

Gabe really didn't know anything about P.J. Foster's whereabouts.

"It was just a chance meeting, and nothing more. He doesn't know anything else," Martin said.

"Let me talk to Gabe and judge for myself what he does and does not know. I know you're trying to protect your son, but I have to do my job. If Gabe can give us even a single lead to go on, I have to question him," she responded.

Penelope opened the door to her office as she called out to Gabe and Alex. She glanced around the room to one of the several places they might be sitting when they were not in the spot she most expected to find them, at the computer. She stepped back into the hallway, a bit surprised, but certain they must have gone down to the other end of the suite of offices where there were a number of vending machines with snacks and sodas.

"I guess the kids must have gotten bored or hungry waiting for us to finish. They're probably down at the other end of the office," she said confidently.

She called out specifically to Alex this time as she rounded the corner and approached a cluster of machines dispensing chips and pretzels to the other unfortunate lawyers and clerks who were stuck in the office on this holiday weekend.

"Hey guys, did any of you see Alex come this way?"

She was now beginning to feel less confident and actually a bit concerned. Martin caught up with her and realized that unless the kids were reviewing law books and legal briefs in the office library, they were no longer on the floor. Given the holiday, most of the other office doors were locked and there was no one at the circular desk in the waiting area.

Martin's heart began to pound in his chest when he remembered that they couldn't have left the building without being noticed by the security guard. What's more, Pete was waiting in the car out on the street in front of the building.

"And besides," he wondered out loud, "Where would they have gone and why?" Gabe could get pretty antsy and didn't have much patience, but he knew he had to meet with the assistant district attorney and at least explain the details of the few hours he had spent sitting next to P.J. Foster on the plane.

"Look, there's no need to worry."

But that was exactly what Gabe's dad was, worried, and trying to imagine Gabe's mom's reaction to his having misplaced their son within the first twenty-four hours of his arrival in the Bad Apple.

"The kids must have gone out to get some air or something. I'm sure they're on their way back up as we speak. Let me call Pete on his cell phone. They might just be hanging out with him in the car waiting until we're finished," Martin said hopefully.

The phone rang a half dozen times when it went to voicemail.

"Pete McDonough's my name. Driving Mr. M. is my game. Now what's your claim to fame?" Martin waited impatiently for the tone so he could leave a message when he finally hung up and dashed out to the elevator.

After what seemed like forever, the elevator stopped and Martin slipped in with Penelope and Jeff right behind him. He pounced on the button marked L for lobby as the doors shut and the car descended the twenty-eight floors to the elaborately decorated atrium.

The three lawyers stopped briefly at the security guard's post to ask whether he had seen the children. He nodded his head affirmatively and pointed to the exit, but before he could explain that they had gotten into the car parked outside and driven away with the young driver, Martin spun through the revolving doors and was out on the street. With no car in sight he pressed redial on his phone, once again trying to reach Pete. He listened to the ridiculous message again, unable to get through to an actual human being and was about to throw the phone down in sheer frustration when the security guard, Penelope, and Jeff tumbled onto the sidewalk through the same revolving doors.

"What's the excitement all about, Ms. Cooper?" the uniformed elderly gentleman asked.

"The kids just went to get some lunch and said to tell you they would be back by the time you finished your meeting. They didn't want to interrupt you so they asked me to give you the message. I tried using the intercom to reach you, but nobody picked up in the office."

"Whew, I guess we got worked up unnecessarily," Penelope said with a renewed calm in her voice. "These are crazy times and we all jumped to a scary conclusion when there was a simple explanation."

Martin was not comforted by either the guard's explanation or Penelope's sense of relief. He did not understand why Pete was not answering his phone, particularly if he had the kids with him. He didn't want to frighten Alex's mom, but suspected that Gabe was up to something and somehow had managed to convince Pete and Alex to go along with him.

"There has to be something more to yesterday's encounter with P.J. Foster that Gabe is not telling me," he muttered to himself. "But what? Why am I letting my imagination run away like this? Why do I always have to be the lawyer rather than the father? Maybe they did all just go out to get some lunch after all."

Chapter Nine

Alex's Plan

The reason Pete hadn't answered either of Martin's frantic calls was that his cell phone was nowhere to be found and he never heard it ring. It was turned off and resting comfortably in Alex's backpack, a maneuver she had managed to pull off as Gabe slipped it into her hand after picking it up from the front passenger seat before settling in the back next to Alex.

"Where is that darn thing? I know I had it with me," Pete said. He checked his pockets and the car's various compartments.

"If I'm taking you guys anywhere, I've got to check it out with your dad, Gabe, and by the way, who might I ask is my new passenger?" Pete inquired.

"Pete, this is Alex, Alex this is Pete," Gabe said very matter of fact like. Clearly, he was not interested in making small talk. He had to come up with some believable explanation to get Pete to help them out without alerting their no doubt panicked parents who were probably already on their trail.

"Okay guys, what are you two up to and just how much trouble am I going to get into for not turning you over to your parents immediately?" Pete asked half-jokingly and half seriously.

"We're not exactly up to anything. We just need some time and a ride uptown to figure out a few things," Gabe admitted.

He hoped that Alex would come up with a better explanation to convince Pete to go along with their not very well planned plan. Alex indeed came to the rescue with just the right balance of fact and fiction to persuade Pete to drive them to the upper west side location of the Kingsley Institute, which she was able to learn from a fairly simple internet search.

For some reason, Gabe had confided in Alex, not only about the encounter with Professor Foster on the plane and the notebook that was left behind, but also that he might have an idea about where Foster went after leaving the airport. Alex checked the location of the Kingsley Institute just before she and Gabe managed to walk out of the office unnoticed by the lawyers preoccupied in the conference room. This was not exactly an archaeological dig, but it would definitely require some pretty cool investigative work to uncover how a 100-year-old inventor got himself into this mess.

Boy, she is good, Gabe thought to himself. He listened to Alex as she filled Pete in about the strange coincidences, the likely kidnapping of P.J. Foster, the imminent danger that the old professor might be in if someone didn't locate him immediately, how long it would take the police to find him with search warrants, probable cause and some other legal procedures that could tie them up for hours, if not days.

Alex's theory was amazingly logical and not at all the way Gabe would have approached the dilemma, logic not being his strong suit. In fact, Gabe had no idea how he would get to the Kingsley Institute until Alex's story unfolded. She actually convinced Pete that if she and Gabe had enough time to reach the Kingsley Institute, they could contact their parents along the way. Martin and Penelope would then have cause to follow them, enter the building without a search warrant, and undoubtedly discover the whereabouts of P.J. Foster. She and Gabe were only temporarily withholding information from their parents to move the investigation of Leonard Harvey's murder along, and to get to the bottom of Professor Foster's involvement.

"Okay, no need to go on. You had me at the possibility that the old guy was kidnapped. These really are a bunch of weird coincidences." Pete started the car, turned west, and headed uptown on his way to West 76th Street and the brownstone where Alex's internet search indicated that the Kingsley Institute was located.

"I knew there was something more that you weren't telling Mr. M. about you and the professor," Pete mumbled to himself. "I knew that you had some idea about where the old guy was heading once he got to New York. It's a good thing that you finally decided to let me in on this, Gabe. I'm not too bad at this sleuthing thing either, you know. Now how about giving me back my phone so I can call your dad? This way I'll let him know you're okay and that I've got this under control," Pete said. He was willing to go along with their plan, just as long as things didn't get out of hand or possibly dangerous.

Pete's attempt to negotiate with his two passengers was cut short, this time not by Alex, but Gabe.

"Just give us enough time to get in the door and scope things out before you call anyone. If Professor Foster is in any danger, the last thing we want to do is turn up at the institute with an army of cops and start a big commotion." Gabe was hoping to postpone the inevitable phone call to his dad as long as possible. Pete seemed convinced, at least for the moment and agreed to hold off on making the call at least until they reached the West 76th Street address of the institute.

The trio of newly minted detectives made it uptown in no time, aided by the unusually light traffic and only an occasional construction detour. As Pete approached the traffic light at Amsterdam Avenue and West 72nd Street, a sudden stream of flashing lights and blaring sirens startled them. No less than ten police cars and assorted fire trucks whizzed past the Volvo, and seemed to be heading, at least by Pete's calculation, straight for the block of the Kingsley Institute, four blocks north of where they were now completely stuck in a total traffic jam.

"Turn down the next street," Gabe pleaded with Pete.

"I can't. There is no way out of this mess, absolutely no place to move this car, right or left," Pete answered in utter frustration. Horns began sounding off from every direction as if drivers imagined they could beep their way out of the tangled web of cars.

"I can't stand this. We've gotta find out what's going on up there," Gabe groaned. He looked to Alex for some possible solution. With that, she opened her backpack, tossed Pete's cell phone to him, unbuckled her seatbelt, and signaled Gabe to open his door, tumbling right on top of him as they landed on the pavement.

Although a bit stunned by this quick maneuver, Gabe stood up and pulled Alex to her feet.

"What now?" he inquired as if there were a choice.

"What now?" Alex repeated knowing that there was no choice, "Follow me and don't worry about Pete. He's got his phone back and I assume you know the number. We'll let him know what's happening as soon as we figure it out," she said.

She was remarkably sure of herself for an archaeologist in training.

Gabe ran north up Amsterdam Avenue with Alex, doing everything he could to keep up as she darted between the cars at one intersection after another. The only way that anything or anyone was moving in this traffic was by foot. And even that was becoming more difficult as crowds of curious onlookers began to gather the closer they got to the corner of West 76th Street.

Gabe suddenly realized that the hand he was holding was no longer Alex's. He was forced to let go a block back when he went right and she went left to avoid crashing into a hot dog vendor. Without looking he grabbed a hand he assumed was Alex's, only to discover he was locking fingers with a strange woman he had never seen before. Gabe quickly let go of the hand and dashed up the block, spotting the bright orange backpack that swung from Alex's shoulder.

They both arrived breathless at the police barricade that was set up to prevent anyone from entering the block of the institute. What they could see, even from this distance, were flames and smoke pouring out of the building. The Kingsley Institute was on fire, with hoses directing torrents of water at the blaze and rescue workers carrying bodies out of the building. His heart pounding so loudly he could hear it in his head, Gabe experienced the first of many instances of heart palpitations and near nervous collapses he would have over the next several hours in the company of Alexandra Cooper. She definitely had far more nerve and courage than any other girl he had ever met before.

Chapter Ten

Where There's Smoke There's Fire

Just as Gabe's dad tried to reach Pete's cell phone for the umpteenth time, he saw the familiar incoming number.

"Thank heavens," he heard himself utter louder than he realized. He and Alex's mom had gone back up to her office on the twenty-eighth floor of the office tower, where he tried to convince himself everything was fine as he practically wore a hole in the carpet from pacing back and forth. He motioned for Penelope to come over to where he was standing and signaled that it must be the kids calling at last.

Alex's mom was not at all pleased that her daughter had gone off without permission. She felt somewhat reassured knowing how level-headed Alex was, and figured that there had to be a logical explanation for her temporary disappearance. Nevertheless, she was relieved to know that Martin's driver was on the phone and that the kids were very likely on their way back.

Her expression of relief quickly disappeared as Martin's face turned ashen and he dropped into the chair behind him.

"What do you mean you don't know where they are?" Penelope heard Martin ask, his voice high pitched and panic-stricken.

"Well, I sort of know where they are," Pete continued on the other end.

"They're on Amsterdam Avenue somewhere between West 72nd and 76th Street."

He offered Gabe's dad the condensed version of the duo's maneuver to get him to drive them to the upper Westside and of their escape into the crowd when they were suddenly stuck in the crush of emergency traffic.

"What are you doing on the upper Westside? What could possibly be happening on West 76th Street?" Martin shouted into the phone. Penelope bent over his shoulder, trying to hear both sides of the conversation.

"I'll tell you what's happening on West 76th Street." Jeff Rogers chimed in from the corridor on his way back from the vending machine with a bag of chips in his hand.

"There's a huge fire in the Kingsley Institute. I just saw the news on my iPad. Isn't that the think tank run by that mind control guru Philip Kingsley?" Jeff added.

He sounded pretty annoyed about having been stuck in the assistant district attorney's office all this time waiting for those bratty kids to show up.

"Let me see that." Martin jumped out of his chair, dropped the cell phone, and grabbed Jeff's iPad.

"Hold on a second, what, are you crazy or something Marty?" Jeff exclaimed.

He refused to let go of the device. As the two lawyers played tug-of-war with the iPad, Alex's mom reached for the office phone and called the 20th precinct.

Sergeant Coburn answered the call and provided Penelope with precisely the information she needed.

There had been a pretty bad fire in the old brownstone that housed the Kingsley Institute early that morning. The NYFD had gotten it under control about a half hour ago. There were a few injuries, but no deaths to report as yet and no one believed trapped or unaccounted for in the building. He would have to check further, but Coburn was fairly certain that there were no children among the injured.

"Okay Marty, as far as I can tell at the moment, with whatever it was that the kids were up to on West 76th Street, they appear to be unharmed, at least from the fire. Now why don't you tell me everything you know and why they were headed up there in the first place," Alex's mom demanded.

This was definitely just about the most serious and severe tone Martin had heard from her all morning.

"I honestly don't know," Gabe's dad responded somewhat awkwardly.

He continued to confess what he now did know from his brief phone conversation with Pete and offered the additional information that not only had Gabe met Professor Foster on the plane from LA, he also apparently knew that Foster had gone to the Kingsley Institute from the airport.

"Your son went off on some misguided adventure knowing full well he could have provided the police with the likely location of a prime murder suspect? What's wrong with him anyway?" Penelope asked accusingly. She backed off a bit when she remembered that her daughter had gone along for the ride too. She wanted to blame the whole thing on Gabe, but for the moment was rather puzzled about why Alex would have agreed to go along. She knew her daughter and was quite convinced that even if it was Gabe's idea to try to find Professor

Foster before the police got to him, it was undoubtedly Alex who planned the escapade to the upper Westside.

While Gabe's dad was upset and embarrassed by this whole mess, he was mostly worried. He found himself frozen in his tracks and unable to think clearly. His visions of a quiet summer holiday weekend at the beach with his son were rapidly spinning out of control and turning into a mid summer's nightmare. He had no idea where Gabe was, if he was safe, or if he had or had not made contact with Professor Foster. He knew Gabe was impulsive, never thought things through before acting, and was probably in way over his head, not to mention in serious danger. What's more, his son had managed to drag the assistant district attorney's daughter into this fiasco, and in less than twenty-four hours had inserted himself and an innocent eleven-year-old girl into a high profile murder investigation. Whoever said that Gabriel Marx was an underachiever?

Penelope, who was caught up in trying to figure out her own next steps to locate her daughter, glanced over to see Martin staring into space as if in a trance. "Marty, I need you to stay focused and work with me. You know the way Gabe thinks and I have a pretty good idea of how Alex's mind works. We have some sense of where the kids are based on Pete's information. We'll find them," she said.

This time she seemed to be trying to reassure Martin more than scold him. She got back on the phone with Sergeant Coburn, gave him the run down on the missing children, and asked to be patched through to the officer in charge at the scene of the fire.

"Detective Santiago here." She heard the officer's voice over the two-way radio and identified herself to him. "We've established a very tight perimeter here, Ms.

Cooper. The rescue workers have removed four casualties, all seriously injured, but expected to survive. No civilians, children or otherwise, have penetrated these barricades since I've been here. The fire inspectors are just completing their work to make certain no one else is in the building and to determine if the structure is still intact in spite of the obvious damage," he reported very officially.

Penelope inquired further to see if the detective could send a patrolman into the crowd of onlookers to check on whether or not the children were still there. Santiago agreed to follow up on her request as soon as someone was available and assured her he would stay on top of the situation.

"We can't just hang around here waiting to hear from the kids," Martin said anxiously. "Can we get a squad car to get us uptown so we can check things out for ourselves?" he asked. He hoped the assistant district attorney could use her considerable clout to get them closer to the actual scene.

"Try calling Pete again. Maybe he's spotted them by now or they've tried to contact him." Penelope insisted.

Gabe's dad attempted to reach the number of his most recently received call when he saw the 310 area code of a new incoming call. This could not possibly be happening, not at this precise moment. Oh yes it could, and it was, for at the exact moment that Gabe's dad had managed to misplace his only son in the middle of a murder investigation in the Bad Apple, Gabe's mom was on the phone, and she was not calling from Los Angeles. Gabe's mom was at that very moment in a cab on her way from JFK airport to Brooklyn. Not that she didn't trust Gabe's dad, which she didn't; not that she wasn't confident that Gabe was being properly supervised in

71

New York, which she wasn't. But when the late night call to Gabe left her somewhat uneasy, she decided it would be a wonderful idea to spend a few days with her somewhat eccentric elderly Uncle Bernard in Brooklyn, a much better vantage point from which to keep an eye on things.

Chapter Eleven

Under Arrest

"Alex, this is crazy," Gabe pleaded. He tried to keep up with his daring new associate and make his way to the front of the growing crowd. "There's no way we're getting any closer to that building. And for all we know, Professor Foster might already have been taken out on one of those stretchers. We don't even know for sure if he was ever there in the first place," Gabe said. While this was a bit unusual for him, Gabe attempted to be sensible for a change.

"Don't be such a wuss, Gabe. You brought me up here for a reason, and we're not leaving until we have some information," Alex replied.

"I don't know who brought who up here, but I think I'm done," Gabe argued. Just then, a very large man stepped in front of him completely blocking his view of the action.

Once again, Gabe was separated from his determined companion, keeping track of her only by the sight of her orange backpack poking through the crowd. "Come on, Alex." He said this in the most take-charge voice he could manage as he tried burrowing his way back to her side. Head down, he pushed his way through the barricade, tumbling onto the other side.

"Touchdown!" the officer exclaimed. She helped Gabe to his feet as the spectators cheered his successful maneuver into the end zone. "Where exactly do you think you're going, young man?" the uniformed female officer inquired.

Somewhat breathless from overshooting his target and making it through the barricade, Gabe stood up to find himself several inches taller than the police officer who looked remarkably familiar to him. Before he could quite figure out why she looked so familiar, Officer Danielli, as her nameplate announced, reached into the crowd and invited Alex to join her and Gabe on the other side of the police divider.

"Just follow me and don't say a word," the officer warned.

"Oh great, we're in for it now," Gabe muttered to Alex. They followed Officer Danielli to an unmarked vehicle parked at the curb just outside of the police perimeter surrounding the scene of the fire.

Detective Santiago had responded to Ms. Cooper's request and asked a patrolman to keep a lookout for the two kids that the assistant district attorney said were missing. When he instructed Officer Nevins to keep an eye out for a 5' 4" twelve-year-old male dressed in jeans and a navy blue UCLA tee-shirt, and a 4'7" eleven-year-old female dressed in khaki shorts, white tank top, and carrying an orange backpack, his colleague, Officer Danielli overheard the exchange and told him not to worry because she would handle it.

As they walked to the car, Gabe couldn't get the thought out of his head that he had seen this police officer before, but where? What was it about her that seemed so familiar?

And then it suddenly hit him. Officer Danielli and the flight attendant who had escorted the professor off the plane and to a cab at JFK airport looked remarkably alike. Could they be, were they in fact the same person?

"I think I know this lady. If she's not the flight attendant who took Professor Foster off the plane, she's her identical twin," Gabe whispered to Alex.

Indeed, one of the last people to see Professor Phineas Jeremiah Foster other than Gabe had apparently reappeared as an NYPD officer. She was no doubt about to arrest him and Alex, and prosecute them to the fullest extent of the law for aiding and abetting an accused felon. And if that weren't bad enough, she would most certainly turn them over to their parents who would just outright kill them.

The block long walk to the car was one of the longest most torturous excursions Gabe had ever made. Visions of his father's endless scolding flashed through his mind, capped off by his mother's getting in on the act only to repeat a million times, "Marty, I told you he was not ready to make this trip alone!"

The only saving grace was that his mother was in Los Angeles and probably wouldn't find out about any of this for a while. Certainly his father would try to keep it from her as long as possible. He knew Dad's life was on the line if Gabe's mom got wind of how he lost his son in the Bad Apple, only to have him picked up by the NYPD for kidnapping an eleven-year-old girl and being an accomplice to murder.

Alex, on the other hand, found this whole thing quite exhilarating and much more intriguing than reviewing recent archaeological digs on the internet. *Nerves of steel, that girl has,* Gabe thought to himself as Officer Danielli opened the rear passenger side door of the car and pointed the way for Gabe and Alex to enter.

"Aren't you going to handcuff us or pat us down?" Alex inquired. She followed Gabe into the back seat of the SUV with blackened side and rear windows. But before Officer Danielli responded, Gabe gasped as he realized that he and Alex were not the only ones in the back seat of the unmarked vehicle.

Once again he found himself seated beside an elderly gentleman he believed he last saw exiting the flight from Los Angeles escorted by the flight attendant, now police officer Danielli. With the exception of the Brooklyn Dodgers baseball cap, which had caught Gabe's attention earlier because it was virtually identical to the one his great Uncle Bernie always wore, Gabe was once again in the company of none other than P.J. Foster.

The last time Gabe remembered hyperventilating quite like this, he had just arrived ten minutes late to his principal's office having run from his middle school's athletic field where he had fallen asleep after a track meet. His parents were seated across from Dr. Jordan's desk with that here we go again look, waiting to discuss his all but having failed one subject report card, his abysmal standardized reading scores, and his complete lack of motivation when it comes to school.

"Relax Gabe, I'll explain everything to you as soon as we get to a secure location," Officer Danielli said. She attempted to calm the obviously completely befuddled almost adolescent.

The old gentleman placed his arm reassuringly around Gabe's shoulders. He smiled warmly at the two children. Officer Danielli sat in the front passenger seat next to a distinguished looking middle-aged man who positioned himself in the driver's seat, started the ignition, and took off heading further uptown.

Unbeknownst to either the driver or any of the passengers in the SUV, they were being followed as they left the scene of the Kingsley Institute fire. Pete McDonough had managed to free himself from the traffic jam on Amsterdam Avenue and pull the Volvo over to the curb just before West 76th Street only feet away from the black unmarked SUV. At first he had no idea what he was witnessing, but when he spotted the orange backpack hanging from the shoulder of one of the passengers entering this rather official looking black Escalade, he started up his engine and wasted no time getting behind it in the now dwindling traffic line-up.

"Hold on Mr. M.," he reported into his cell phone. "I've spotted the kids and I'm on it. I'll be back in touch as soon as we land."

Chapter Twelve

Mistaken Identity

Officer Danielli was neither a New York City police officer nor a transcontinental flight attendant. She was in fact Danielle Foster, the daughter of Dr. Jonas Foster, recently deceased archaeologist, and great granddaughter of the very much alive, although somewhat worn out from the last forty-eight hours, Professor Phineas Jeremiah Foster.

This was of course no mere coincidence, as Officer Danielli, alias Danielle Foster, had carefully planned to seat her famous great grandfather next to Gabe once they boarded the jumbo jet from Los Angeles to New York the day before. Flight attendant and police officer uniforms, fake security badges and IDs were just a few among the many disguises and accessories that Ms. Foster kept on hand since going undercover for the National Institute of Brain Science, better known as NIBS.

NIBS had recruited her under the pretense that it was investigating the increasing number of unmotivated, unenthusiastic, apathetic, underachieving students throughout the country. Once she had confirmed her great grandfather's involvement in the project, she agreed to take on the assignment.

Unfortunately, NIBS had duped both the professor and Danielle. NIBS, under the direction of Dr. Philip Kingsley, had never intended to help young people. Its intention was quite the opposite, to manipulate and control them through various experimental procedures that promised considerable financial gain. Unaware of its true mission, P.J. Foster emerged from seclusion after thirty years to resume the work he had abandoned.

While he had not been heard from publicly for decades, NIBS operatives learned that P.J. Foster had been collecting school records and personal profiles on thousands of children around the country. They knew that the professor had developed experimental devices, and conducted research as part of his lifelong commitment to give every child a chance to triumph.

Foster had his critics, those who accused him of being a fraud, nothing more than a high tech cheat. Kingsley, on the other hand, saw the opportunity to exploit the eccentric old professor.

If P.J. Foster needed a bona fide unmotivated, unenthusiastic, apathetic, underachieving student to continue his research, then he would have one. And that was where Gabriel Marx figured into all of this.

The professor had no interest in profit and mind control. His desire was only to help these so-called underachievers to feel worthy, to restore their self-esteem. But unbeknownst to him, there were those who were interested only because of the power and financial windfall they anticipated at the expense of turning school children into experimental subjects.

The professor had flown from Geneva, Switzerland to Los Angeles to attend his grandson's memorial service two weeks ago. That was just about the same time that he had identified Gabriel Marx from his huge database as the best possible candidate for his research. With Danielle under contract to NIBS, he had the help he needed to secure Gabe's involvement. Danielle had also arrived in LA for her father's funeral, and planned the airplane encounter which would bring them all to New York.

Two days after the funeral, the professor learned that Gabe would be flying to New York to spend the summer with his father. How did the professor obtain all of this valuable surveillance? Danielle Foster, of course! What would he have done without his ever curious, faithful, charming, and somewhat devious great granddaughter?

Danielle had booked the professor on the same flight as Gabe and managed to switch his originally assigned seat so that the contact could be made. That was the easy part. The tricky part came next. She bet on the fact that Gabe's curiosity would get the better of him and that once he recognized the old man, and discovered the notebook, he'd become intrigued and try to find him after he vanished from the airport so mysteriously.

What Danielle had not counted on was that her father's death in Egypt would be ruled a probable homicide, and her great grandfather would become the prime suspect in a high profile murder case within hours after arriving in New York. What did these two things have in common? The answer was quite simple--Philip Kingsley.

"Great Gramps," Danielle repeatedly warned the old man. "I know that NIBS is providing the funds you need to continue your work, but do you really trust that creep, Kingsley? He's only interested because of the dollar signs he sees at the end of all of this. He couldn't care less about the kids. For him it's the profit, first, second, and last," she insisted.

The old man tried to convince Danielle that it was more than the money. "Kingsley has the resources, the connections, and the money," he argued. "I need him as much as he needs me," he continued. Although Danielle was never persuaded, her love and trust in the old man won out. She offered her considerable talent and training as a military intelligence officer, a uniform she actually had worn legitimately several years ago, to her great grandfather.

The SUV slowed to a stop at the intersection as the driver glanced repeatedly into his rear view mirror. "Someone's following us," he reported calmly. "Do you want me to lose him?' he inquired.

Without any expression of worry or concern in her voice, Danielle asked, "Is it a white Volvo sedan?"

Gabe and Alex looked at each other, half relieved and half panicked at the thought that they were about to be overtaken by Pete McDonough. He certainly deserved credit for hanging in there and tracking them down after all of this time.

"No, just make him think you're trying to lose him. Let's make it a little suspenseful and challenging for him so that when he finds us, he actually thinks he earned his pay as a super sleuth," Danielle replied.

"Who's following us, Danielle?" the professor asked, somewhat puzzled.

"Pete McDonough, Martin Marx's driver and an accomplice in the children's escape from the assistant district attorney's office," Danielle answered.

"Isn't that a bit risky, my dear?" the professor continued. "Isn't it likely that he'll try to contact Gabe's father and no doubt bring the police to our very doorstep?" he went on.

"Not the Pete McDonough I know," Danielle said reassuringly.

"You know this man, this Pete, Danielle?" the professor continued his line of questioning.

"Yes, Great Gramps, and so do you," Danielle replied. She was somewhat surprised at the old man's reaction.

Perhaps his age is finally getting the better of him, she thought when her great grandfather, who never forgot a thing, didn't recall the part that Pete had unknowingly played in their locating Gabe in the first place. But if Danielle was a little surprised, the two young passengers seated on either side of the old man were downright relieved to know that Pete was on their trail.

Chapter Thirteen

Great Uncle Bernard

Little did Gabe know that while he and Alex were being taken who knows where, his mother was only a few miles away. Gabe's mom could barely catch her breath as she reached the fourth floor of Uncle Bernard's walk up apartment building. "How does the old guy do this every day? He has to be close to eighty by now," she said, as she dragged her suitcase up the final step. She inhaled the familiar smells of the old building, and reached for the doorbell. No doubt about it. She had arrived at Uncle Bernard's apartment.

There was no mistaking the wafting aroma of some concoction he was cooking in anticipation of her return to the old neighborhood. Gabe's mom had many fond memories of her childhood in Brooklyn, and among her favorite recollections were her times with Uncle Bernard.

The door opened. Two outstretched arms extending beyond the grease-spattered apron that hung from her uncle's neck greeted Elly. Hugs don't get any better than Uncle Bernard's. And today this particular hug was a welcome relief from a sleepless night on the redeye from

LA and a hike up four flights of stairs, not to mention an uneasy feeling in the pit of her stomach about Gabe.

"Sweetie, I was thrilled when you called and said you wanted to come for a visit. It's been how long now, more than a year at least? Where's that kid of yours? Isn't Gabe with you?" Bernard asked. He glanced around the corridor, expecting to see his great nephew appear from behind the hallway column.

"No, he's not with me. He's with his father for the summer. This is the first trip he's made east by himself and quite honestly, call it mother's intuition or something, I'm worried about him," Elly replied. She tried to explain her sudden appearance in a city that she stayed away from as much as possible.

It wasn't that Gabe's mom hated New York as much as she didn't trust it. And more importantly, she didn't trust Gabe in this city without her. She knew he needed to spend time with his father, but wished he didn't have to travel three thousand miles to see him, custody agreement or not. But whose crazy idea was it to let Gabe come by himself this time?

"He's almost a teenager, Elly. You've got to cut the apron strings sooner or later. He's ready to fly by himself. In fact, it will do him some good and give him a sense of independence. School problems or not, he's got a good head on his shoulders. He can do this — we can do this. Give him a chance to feel a little grown up," Gabe's dad had pleaded with her over and over again.

"Come on, Mom, you keep promising, please." Elly recalled Gabe begging her to let him make the trip unaccompanied.

"But you hate flying, Gabe. Are you really sure you're ready to do this alone?" She asked him at least fifty times a day until she finally gave in and agreed to let his father make the airline reservations.

Gabe was not any surer than his mother that going alone was a good idea, but he knew how much it meant to his dad. It was something he had to prove, not only to his dad, but to himself.

Well, Elly may have let Gabe fly to New York by himself, but it wasn't more than twenty-four hours later and the first available flight into JFK that she followed close behind. Well, not too close, she rationalized, since Gabe would be out on Long Island with his father and she would visit her childhood Brooklyn neighborhood and her seemingly ageless Uncle Bernard. "What is it about that man? Everyone seems to get older while he gets younger each year," she heard herself say whenever she thought of him.

It wasn't that he didn't look as if he were in his eighth decade, with his almost completely bald head and gray beard covering his deeply lined face. It was his attitude, his demeanor, his zest for living. He was forever adolescent in his excitement about everything. Well, why not? He loved his work, although Elly still was not quite sure that he ever had a real job. He had never married and more importantly, he never had any kids. What did he have to worry about?

By Elly's calculations, there would be exactly one hundred and fifteen miles between her and Gabe, not perfect, but much better than three thousand.

"Elly, what are you worried about? He's fine." Bernard tried to reassure her as he returned to the stove. "Put your suitcase in the other room and come into the kitchen so we can catch up," he said with his usual boyish enthusiasm.

Gabe's mom walked down the narrow hallway, its walls covered with old family photos. This had been her grandparents' apartment where her father and his older brother Bernard had grown up, where she had spent hours as a child fascinated by Bernard's story telling. But that was decades earlier and of all those pictured on the walls, the only one who remained on Windsor Place, Brooklyn, New York was Bernard Marshall. All the others had died or moved to Florida or Arizona or in her case California. Bernard was the last remaining connection to her past with its mostly happy memories. He was the last remaining connection to New York except for Gabe's father who returned there after the divorce, forcing her to face the anxiety-ridden separations from her son.

Elly deposited her suitcase in one of the three bedrooms, took a few minutes to wash up, and joined her uncle in the kitchen. "Okay Uncle Bernie, you're right. There is probably absolutely nothing to worry about. Gabe is with his dad, a reliable and successful attorney, who is perfectly capable of managing his son for a few weeks," Elly said. She almost managed to convince herself. "But if everything is alright, why hasn't Marty answered his cell phone since I got into town this morning?" she asked. Once again, she doubted that Gabe's father could balance all of the things that were needed to parent their sometimes challenging son.

Gabe's mom sat at the kitchen table while Bernard put the finishing touches on his version of chicken soup. "I know its chicken soup, but you've got to put a chunk of pot roast in it to give it the real flavor." He flourished his arms in midair as if he were taping an episode for the Food Channel. Elly began to relax, comfortable in the kitchen that held so many childhood memories. She glanced across the room where a copy of the daily paper rested on an unused countertop.

Elly reached for the newspaper, read the headline, and had all the evidence she needed to strengthen her case against the city. "You see Uncle Bernie, first thing you see when you pick up the paper in this town, murder, murder, and more murder," she declared. Gabe's mom read the headline out loud to prove her point. As she got to the third line in the article, the one describing the murder victim, Leonard Harvey, as having been indicted for fraud and represented by the law firm of Marx and Rogers, she dropped the paper and began searching frantically for her cell phone.

Bernard tried to catch the objects rapidly flying out of Elly's purse as she hunted for her cell phone. "What are you doing, Elly?" he asked. He was puzzled by her even more frantic than usual hysteria. "Sweetie, calm down. What's wrong?" He tried to understand what had triggered this sudden outburst. Almost breathless, she managed to combine a few scattered syllables with a sequence of gestures and finger pointing to the words in the newspaper.

By the time Elly located her phone, Bernard realized what had set her off. Gabe's father was involved in a high profile murder investigation, which probably explained why he wasn't answering his phone. But where did that leave Gabe? Well, for once maybe Elly really did have something to worry about.

Elly tried repeatedly to reach Gabe's dad on his cell phone, finally resorting to texting as a desperate measure. Bernard sat by her side, but could do very little to comfort her. He picked up the newspaper and read a bit further, until he too was stunned by what he read. He spoke the words out loud so that he could hear as well as see what he thought had to be a bizarre coincidence, an outrageous mistake. "Phineas Jeremiah Foster, renowned inventor and recluse is being sought as the prime suspect in the murder investigation of Leonard Harvey."

Bernard stood up as Elly attempted to contact Marty over and over again. He walked to the hallway, to the wall of photos that depicted his life story. He knew exactly which one he was looking for and when he found it, removed it from the wall, his hands uncharacteristically trembling. It was as if he had seen or at least heard from or about a ghost. He stared at the framed picture in his hand, the one dated July 1939, the one of his father and mother with their old friend Phinny, and on Phinny's shoulders, a small child, four-year-old Bernard.

Seventy-five years later, that child, now almost eighty-year-old Great Uncle Bernard, began to put together the pieces, dig through his own past, and figure out if Elly really had any reason to be worried about Gabe. With his mind racing through scenes from the last eight decades — Brooklyn, the lab, the experiments, Phineas's daughters, Europe, and back to Brooklyn, he knew there was little time to spare. Not only might Gabe be in serious trouble, his old friend and mentor, Phinny, was probably in grave danger!

Chapter Fourteen

Family Album

"Uncle Bernie, what's wrong? You look like you've just seen a ghost." The old man emerged from the hallway clinging to the photograph he had removed from the wall.

"Elly, this P.J. Foster who the police are looking for, you've heard of him, haven't you?" Uncle Bernie asked, his voice unusually serious.

"Not really," Gabe's mom replied. "Who is he?"

"Well for one thing, he's the prime murder suspect in the death of Gabe's father's client, Leonard Harvey," Uncle Bernie explained. "For another, he's one of the most famous inventors in the world. But more important that any of that, he was your grandfather's best friend. If not for Phinny Foster, I wouldn't be standing here or anywhere else today. He was like a second father to me."

With that as an introduction, Gabe's mom learned things about her family and her Uncle Bernie that she could hardly believe. The facts that were revealed to her about Uncle Bernie and his connection to Professor Foster briefly distracted her from her quest to locate her son. And indeed, it was her son, Gabriel Marx, who was now smack in the middle of this unfolding family drama, not to mention murder mystery.

There was one thing Uncle Bernie was absolutely certain about. P.J. Foster did not murder anyone, not deliberately, not accidentally, not at all. He was equally certain someone was trying to frame the professor for the murder, to discredit him once and for all. Someone was definitely out to ruin his reputation, and possibly do him great harm.

"When was the last time that you saw the professor?" Elly asked her uncle.

"I haven't seen him in over thirty years, not since his daughter died in a car accident," Uncle Bernie replied. There was a deep sadness in his voice. "That was when he broke off contact with the outside world, and particularly with me.

"Why you? He was your mentor, your idol from everything you've told me." Gabe's mom was now even more confused.

"Because I was driving the car. If I hadn't insisted on taking a drive that morning, P.J. Foster's daughter wouldn't have died that day. He never forgave me and I never forgave myself," Uncle Bernie explained. He spoke the words as if he were experiencing the pain of the tragedy all over again after all of these years.

"Wait, wait, wait," Elly insisted. "There's more to this than you're telling me," she said. She thought about her own childhood. She would have been around eight years old when the accident occurred. Certainly she would remember hearing something about it. "Why haven't I heard anything about this before?" Elly asked, becoming all the more curious about her uncle's apparent secret life.

That was when Uncle Bernie completed the story for his niece, the story he was certain he would take to the grave, the story he had given his word to P.J. Foster never to speak of again. But it was precisely this story which Uncle Bernie had to tell now. It was the story which would prove to the world that Phineas Jeremiah Foster was no murderer. It was the story, which by telling, might yet renew his relationship with his old friend and mentor.

"P.J. Foster and his wife had two children, identical twin daughters born just around the time the photo was taken of me sitting on Phinny's shoulders over seventy-five years ago. I was just four years old. I grew up with the girls and spent most of my childhood getting into one kind of mischief or another in the professor's makeshift basement laboratory. We were the guinea pigs for his research and the first to try out whatever new-fangled invention he was working on," Uncle Bernie explained.

"Life was quite ideal for all of us until one of the twins, Rose, became seriously ill with an unexplained high fever. The fever was followed by a series of seizures, each one more devastating than the one before. The doctors believed her death was certain, but miraculously she pulled through under the constant watch of her father who rarely left her bedside," Uncle Bernie continued.

"Rose survived what turned out to be scarlet fever, but was never the same. She barely spoke and had difficulty doing even the most basic things for herself. If P.J. Foster had been dedicated to children before his daughter's illness, he was evermore so after her recovery. He worked tirelessly, yet despite his success with other children, there was little he could do for Rose. He enlisted the help of his other daughter, Julia, and of course the girls' favorite playmate, me, so that Rose would be included in all of our escapades. The professor was determined to make her life as normal as possible. But her life was never normal again, and neither were our lives.

"I loved the role of adopted big brother, but Julia became more and more jealous of all of the attention lavished on her broken sister. Childhood turned into adolescence and Julia became even more bitter. Her anger was only temporarily calmed by her growing affection for me and the promise that we would marry when she turned twenty-one."

"But Uncle Bernie, you were never married, were you?" Elly asked. She was quite certain that there had never been any mention of an Aunt Julia.

"No, when the professor left for Geneva, Switzerland, to take a research position at the university, I agreed to go along as his assistant. That outraged Julia even more and she broke our engagement," Uncle Bernie explained.

"Those were the missing years, Elly, the years I lived in Europe, traveling with the professor, his wife, and Rose. I dabbled, but never married. The work was too compelling. I was hooked, but not on Julia," Uncle Bernie continued.

"Did you have any more contact with Julia after that?" Elly inquired further.

"No one did. She virtually disappeared," Uncle Bernie replied. "There was some talk that she had a child. I must admit I even thought that I might have been the father, but she clearly wanted nothing else to do with me, and so I gave up any fantasy about that. After those years in Europe, I returned to the states. That was probably just after you were born, Elly. I moved back in with Mama and Papa, your grandparents, and got to be your favorite uncle," he said, his sense of humor returning to his voice.

"But what about the car accident? When does that figure into all of this?" Gabe's mom asked.

"The professor contacted me about eight years later, sounding pretty shaken up. His wife had died and he was trying to balance his work and care for Rose at the same time. He asked me to return to Geneva to assist him with a special project," Uncle Bernie answered. "I wasn't doing anything particularly interesting at the time, so I agreed. That was when I found out that his work was being discredited, that he had received threatening letters and that there had even been an attempt on his life. He needed me to look after Rose until what he called, 'this nonsense', blew over," Bernard explained. The look of deep sadness returned to his face.

"Elly, there was a car crash, but it was no accident. We were forced off the road. There was never any doubt in my mind or in the professor's," Uncle Bernie continued as his emotions went from grief to rage. The rest of the story came into focus as Bernard Marshall concluded, his voice sounding more and more helpless.

"I managed to crawl out of the crumbled vehicle, but with no cell phones and in a remote area, Rose didn't stand a chance.

"The professor went into seclusion. His work stopped. I returned to the states. The authorities never identified the driver who had forced my fragile passenger and me off the road. An investigation into the death threats the professor had received ended without answers, except for the nagging suspicion that has haunted me every day of my life since. Yes, I am quite certain that P.J. Foster hasn't murdered anyone, but I have a pretty good idea who did and why."

"So now what?" Gabe's mom asked frantically.

"The paper says the professor is missing. The police may not know where he is, but if he's back in New York, I may know how to find him," Uncle Bernie answered. "There's no need to worry. There's no reason to believe that Gabe is involved in this at all. I'm sure whatever Marty's role is; he's kept his son out of any murder investigation."

"Uncle Bernie, Marty has not answered his phone for hours. Gabe has a sixth sense for trouble. We're in the middle of New York City, where anything that can go wrong usually does, and you actually expect me to believe that Gabe is not in the middle of this? Call it mother's intuition or everyday neurosis, but I have no doubt that Gabe is smack in the middle of this mess," Elly said, growing more hysterical with each word.

Chapter Fifteen

Innocent Until Proven Guilty

"Pete, don't you dare hang up on me," Gabe's father shouted into the phone. "Where exactly are you?" But before he could finish his question, the phone went dead.

"Either Pete hung up or we lost the signal," Gabe's dad explained to Alex's mom as they sat in the back seat of the squad car heading uptown.

Penny instructed the officer who was driving to head to the West 76th Street location of the Kingsley Institute. "I'm sure the police at the scene have tracked the kids down by now, although it is a bit strange that we haven't heard back from them yet," Penny said, somewhat puzzled. "Let me try to reach Detective Santiago again."

Martin didn't know how much longer he could avoid answering Gabe's mom's phone calls. There were at least seven frenzied messages from her that he had managed to ignore. But when the phone signaled her text, he knew he couldn't put off responding much longer. He redialed Pete's number and got that stupid message of his again as his frustration and his blood pressure reached a peak.

Penny reached Detective Santiago on the two-way radio, but he was no help. "Nope, Ms. Cooper. I sent an officer into the crowd to look for the kids, but no luck. There is no way they are still hanging around up here or we would have located them by now." The detective in charge was quite certain that his officers had been thorough in their search.

"Marty, Santiago says that there is no sign of the kids anywhere near the Kingsley Institute. You've got to reach Pete. He is apparently the only one who has actually seen them since they left the office three hours ago. Whether they found who or what they were looking for is anyone's guess, but there is no one left inside the brownstone on West 76th," Penny explained.

"My guess is that if Foster was ever at the Institute, he either got out before the fire started or he's lying in a hospital somewhere in the city. I'm going to find out where the victims were taken and if any of them have been identified yet," she continued, trying to organize her thoughts. Her first priority was Alex, but she couldn't lose sight of the Harvey murder investigation and her prime suspect, P.J. Foster.

Penny put in another call to Santiago and learned that the fire victims, all four of them, were taken to the burn unit at University Hospital. It was now believed that among the victims were a secretary, a research assistant, Philip Kingsley himself, and an unidentified elderly man. "That's it! We've got Foster. It has to be him," Penny exclaimed. For a moment, she forgot that while she might possibly have located P.J. Foster, her daughter was still missing.

Gabe's dad tried to figure out his next move. Another call to Pete, continue to drive around Manhattan looking for Gabe like a needle in a haystack, or finally respond to Elly and confess all that had happened since Gabe's arrival?

"Do you still want me to drive you to the Kingsley Institute, Ms. Cooper?" the police officer asked, uncertain of his own next move.

"No. Make your way to University Hospital," she responded quite emphatically, "If we can get a positive ID on the old guy they took out of the building, that will settle that. Radio Santiago again, and make sure that they've posted a police guard at the burn unit. I want to talk to the old man as soon as the doctors say it's okay," Penny said. She took charge of the situation as best she could under the circumstances.

Alex's mom was convinced that not only was she minutes away from taking her murder suspect into custody, she also felt confident that the kids might be somewhere near the hospital trying to stay close to Foster as well.

Gabe's dad, on the other hand, was still frozen in indecision and welcomed any action at this point, as long as he could postpone contact with Gabe's mom.

The cell phone ring startled both of them as they just about knocked heads trying to hear the voice on the other end. "Hey Mr. M., where are you?" Pete asked in a surprisingly casual tone.

"Where am I? Where are you for heaven's sake? Do you have the kids?" Martin fired back at him.

"Not exactly, but I know where they are and it's cool," he said, trying to reassure his boss.

"What do you mean you know where they are? Where are they, Pete?" Gabe's dad demanded.

Pete explained that he followed the black Escalade to an address on West 86th Street, right off of Central Park, where Gabe, Alex, a police officer, and an old man in a wheelchair entered the building. "I'm keeping a safe distance, Mr. M., like a regular detective, but I'd recognize that orange backpack anywhere," Pete said proudly. "They're with that old Foster guy. I'm sure of it," Pete continued, sounding certain.

Gabe's dad turned to Alex's mom. "Well, either your prime suspect is in the burn unit at University Hospital, or he's unharmed and hosting Gabe and Alex at some apartment on the Upper Westside. Take your pick," Marty said, inviting Penny to choose what to do next.

"Hold on, Mr. M. Oh man, this sucks, I think she spotted me." Just then, Officer Danielli, alias Danielle Foster, approached the white Volvo sedan parked at the fire hydrant across from the building she had just exited.

Once again, the phone went dead, but only for a minute as it sounded off with that very distinctive ring that could only mean one thing. Gabe's mom was on the other end and this time Martin had no choice. He had to take the call. Unusually composed and by this time much less hysterical, Elly simply asked, "Marty, is Gabe with you?"

"Not exactly," Martin nervously replied to Gabe's mom.

"I didn't think so. I'm not sure how you managed to lose Gabe in the little more than twenty-four hours he's been with you, but we may know where he is," Elly said.

Martin, now totally baffled, was in no position to argue with Gabe's mom. "Okay Elly, where do you think he is, and where are you for that matter? And what do you mean we?" he asked.

"Never mind where I am. What I can tell you is that P. J. Foster didn't murder Leonard Harvey or anybody else for that matter. But Uncle Bernie has a pretty good idea who did and why."

"Uncle Bernie, your uncle Bernie? What does he have to do with... wait a minute, how did you know about P.J. Foster or the murder of Leonard Harvey?" Gabe's dad inquired, somewhat stunned.

"Don't you read the papers or listen to the news, Marty? What I don't quite understand is how you got your son involved in this mess," Elly responded.

"Me, you can't blame this one on me. This is something Gabe managed to accomplish very much on his own. That kid is no underachiever when it comes to trouble," Martin said. He was having trouble concealing his frustration, let alone his humiliation that Elly might figure out where Gabe was before he did.

Chapter Sixteen

Reunion

"Pete McDonough, of all people to run into. What a coincidence, Peter!" Danielle exclaimed.

"What are you doing here, Dan…?" Pete began and stopped suddenly mid sentence realizing that the police officer who escorted Gabe and Alex to the black unmarked Escalade was none other than Danielle Foster.

"Wait just a minute," he continued, finding his voice again. "This has got to be some kind of bad joke. You can't possibly be related to the Foster that half of the NYPD is looking for, can you?" he asked.

"I can and I am," she answered.

That was Pete's aha moment. Doc, the sweet old man who occasionally visited his great granddaughter Danielle was the most sought-after murder suspect in New York. In the excitement of the last two days, Pete had not managed to put two and two together, that is not until this very moment as Danielle Foster appeared before him all decked out like a New York City cop.

"I wondered where you had gone off to, Peter," Danielle said, referring to Pete's somewhat sudden departure from his job as a doorman in her west village apartment building.

"You wondered where I had gone off to? It's not Halloween, Danielle. Why are you dressed up like that, and what is going on here anyway?" Pete responded, turning the questioning around.

"You first, Pete," Danielle insisted.

"Well, I didn't exactly leave on my own. I was fired for taking too much time off," Pete confessed. "I needed the time to finish up some long overdue work so that I could go back to school. I thought I might actually have a shot at finishing college. But that was a total bust because in the end I wound up screwing up on the job and in school. The only saving grace was that Mr. M., took me on full time as his driver," Pete explained.

"Mr. M., as in Mr. Martin Marx, father of Gabriel Marx, as in the young man currently on his way to my great grandfather's lab? That Mr. M.?"

With that, Pete realized that Danielle Foster knew way too much about his current employer, but how? He was now completely puzzled by the coincidences, and wondered if he was somehow responsible for getting Gabe into this mess.

As the back and forth interrogation went on between Peter and Danielle, Gabe and Alex stepped out of the elevator, which rather than having gone up, descended to a sub basement level in the building. They followed the old man as he rolled his wheelchair into the cavernous underground space. There they were greeted by several lab coated technicians and someone who seemed to be in charge.

"Children, let me introduce you to my grandson, Dr. Jonas Foster," the professor announced. Gabe and Alex looked at each other as if they had just seen a ghost, which according to the website they had checked a few hours ago, they had.

"Don't look so shocked, kids; the reports of my death were greatly exaggerated. I am indeed very much alive," the younger of the Fosters proclaimed.

Gabe and Alex barely had time to be stunned by this latest revelation when they were escorted to an inner chamber surrounded by a maze of glass-paneled workspaces. Each was occupied by a computerized figure masquerading as a child, but not just any child. Each of these remarkably authentic looking pre-teen robots bore an uncanny resemblance to none other than Gabe himself.

For the first time since his arrival in New York, Gabe's excitement at his unexpected adventure turned to downright panic. He couldn't decide what was worse, being in the company of a murder suspect, a dead man, and a dozen computer driven clones of himself, or explaining to his father how he got into this predicament. Thankfully he didn't have to deal with his mother just yet, with her back in Los Angeles some three thousand miles away. At least, that was what he thought. He had no idea that she and Uncle Bernie were already in hot pursuit.

Alex, on the other hand, couldn't have been any happier. Her bravado seemed to grow with every twist and turn since she and Gabe left her mother's office. "So you faked your death, Dr. Foster," she announced. "No doubt you used some sort of herbal sedative which put you into such a deep state of relaxation that you appeared dead," she added, much to the surprise of the scientists in the room.

"Impressive, my dear," responded Jonas Foster. "You clearly are familiar with various ancient tribal practices. Not too many experienced archaeologists know about such things, let alone a novice such as yourself. Impressive indeed," Dr. Foster repeated, glancing somewhat furtively at his grandfather.

"But how did you fake the autopsy, Dr. Foster?" Alex continued her questioning. "The website reported that an autopsy had been done and that you died of an apparent heart attack."

"Well, my budding young scientist, first rule of evidence. Don't believe everything you read on the internet. False postings are easy enough to plant. Separating fact from fiction, well that's another matter," he concluded, turning his attention to his grandfather.

The elder Foster smiled in return, but seemed somewhat uneasy about the whole situation. "Jonas, shouldn't Danielle have joined us by now?" the professor asked. He was obviously quite nervous about Danielle's absence.

"I have no doubt that she has the situation under control. I'm sure she'll be down here any minute with Mr. McDonough in tow," his grandson replied.

"Just the same, I would feel much better if we were all here together so that we could proceed to the next phase of our work," the professor insisted, seeming increasingly anxious. "If young Pete has managed to contact the children's parents, the authorities might locate us at any moment. I could be arrested for Leonard Harvey's murder and we both know what that would mean."

No sooner had the professor expressed his concern about his great granddaughter's whereabouts, than the elevator door opened. The professor looked up, somewhat startled. Rather than the young twosome he had expected, in walked a strangely familiar acquaintance.

Gabe could hardly believe his eyes as his great uncle entered the room. "What is Uncle Bernie doing here? And if he's here, that means my mother can't be too far behind. Oh, now I'm really in for it," Gabe exclaimed, as Bernard Marshall came into view through the glass partition. "How did my mom find us when the entire NYPD couldn't?"

Gabe always knew that his mother had outstanding radar when it came to tracking him down, but this was good even for her. But it was not Gabe who Bernard Marshall approached first. As the professor struggled to lift himself out of his wheelchair, Uncle Bernie reached out to embrace his old mentor.

Uncle Bernie then turned his attention to the children and quite certain about what Gabe must be thinking, reassured him that his mother was not lurking outside. "It wasn't easy young man, but I managed to convince her to stay put in the apartment in Brooklyn," Uncle Bernie explained.

"Brooklyn, what is she doing in Brooklyn?" Gabe asked.

"You know your mother, Gabe. Exactly how long do you think she could last in LA knowing you were in New York?" Uncle Bernie replied.

"How did you find me, Bernard?" the professor interrupted. He was obviously surprised by this unexpected reunion.

"You may have ordered me out of your life thirty years ago, my friend, but that doesn't mean I no longer know how your mind works. I'm not sure how you got involved with this Leonard Harvey character, Phinny, but I have a pretty good idea who is behind all of this."

Gabe stared at his great uncle in utter amazement, now feeling less frightened, but even more confused.

Alex, as courageous as ever, was equally puzzled by these most recent developments. She had no idea who Uncle Bernie was, but soon learned that he knew more about P.J. Foster than just about anyone. More importantly, he knew how to find P.J. Foster, and he knew that the professor would successfully elude the police by retreating to the depths of his underground laboratory on the upper west side of Manhattan.

But there were still many things that Gabe didn't understand. He didn't know that Uncle Bernie was much less concerned about the police and the murder charge than most everyone else trying to track down P.J. Foster. Gabe had no idea that the professor faced a far worse dilemma. He knew nothing about Uncle Bernie's past connection to the professor, or the revenge being sought by his daughter, Julia. Gabe didn't realize that the real challenge would be preventing the old man's estranged daughter from destroying her father. Bernard Marshall knew what the professor's daughter was after, and that she would not rest until she sabotaged P.J. Foster's research and put a stop to his life's work once and for all.

Chapter Seventeen

Here a Gabe, There a Gabe, Everywhere a Gabe

Phineas Foster examined the look on Bernard's face, and considered how his entry into the current situation might complicate matters. He had a pretty good idea what Bernard must be thinking, and knowing how familiar he was with the Foster family history, was quite certain that his instincts were right on target.

For Uncle Bernie, it was clear. Somehow Julia had managed to insert herself into the professor's life again, if only to see that it ended in the disgrace she believed her father deserved. It was of no consequence to her that she would destroy decades of vital research precisely at the moment when the professor was on the brink of the breakthrough he knew was only weeks, if not days away.

"Well my friends, we have no time to lose," the professor declared. "We shall complete our work here in short order. This is not how I expected to conclude the project, but given the events of the last two days, there is no choice but to change our course of action. If young Master Marx is ready to proceed, let's get on with it."

"Who is he talking about? Does he mean me Alex?" Gabe asked anxiously. He didn't always listen very closely when adults were talking to him or about him, but Phineas Foster now had his full attention.

"I'm pretty sure he means you, Gabe," Alex whispered. She was actually excited about the uncertainty of what was to follow and a bit disappointed that the professor hadn't invited her to participate.

"Wait, don't you need parental consent or something to use me as a guinea pig?" Gabe insisted. He remembered all of the times his mother signed the papers so that he could be tested or tutored by one expert after another.

"Strictly speaking, we do," Professor Foster answered. "But that was when we thought we would be finishing this project at the Kingsley Institute and that Dr. Philip Kingsley could have persuaded your father to give his consent. We're under very different pressure right now, and there is no time to lose over details like that," the professor explained.

Alex did not like the sound of that at all. The excitement she experienced a moment ago suddenly shifted. She couldn't quite explain her uneasiness about what Professor Foster had just said, but it sounded a lot like Gabe didn't have any choice about whether or not to participate. These scientists weren't particularly interested in Gabe. They were interested in their results, no matter what they had to do to get them. More importantly, the audience of lifeless Gabe-like robots that surrounded them was beginning to spook her out.

"Gabe, there is no need to worry," the professor's grandson, Jonas Foster, interrupted.

"Please grandfather, let's take this a little slower and explain things to the boy and his friend more clearly," Jonas Foster continued.

"Certainly, you know we would never do anything to harm you or any child for that matter. Perhaps in our haste, we have failed to explain just how critical this work is to all children," Jonas Foster said reassuringly. He spoke in a much gentler and persuasive manner, and was rather stunned at how uncharacteristically forceful his grandfather had been with the young boy.

Professor Foster picked up the cue from his grandson and changed the tone and intensity of his voice.

"We've been through a great deal in the last forty-eight hours," he said, more gently this time. We thought my arrival in New York would go unnoticed. And while we did expect that you would eventually locate me at the Kingsley Institute, Gabe, we never imagined that it would be in the middle of a murder investigation and the near destruction of the place."

"Well, we all know who must have been behind that," Uncle Bernie interjected. "There is no telling what more havoc Julia will cause on her mission to destroy you, Phinny," he warned. "But wait a minute. The boy is right. What makes you think I would simply let you experiment on him, let alone convince him to participate?" Uncle Bernie said. "I think even you may have gone too far this time with your obsession to make the perfect child, to control what you were unable to control with Rose seventy years ago."

"Julia, Rose, who are these people and what do they have to do with me anyway?" Gabe exploded. He was no longer able to stand by quietly waiting for these scientists to do who knows what to him.

"I'm out of here, guys. I don't know what you're up to or why, and frankly I don't care. I am sick and tired of people thinking they have to fix me to fit what they think I have to be like, think like, act like. If it's not my mother, it's my father, or my teachers, and now you, a bunch of white coats with Ph.D.s who want to make me into someone or something I'm not. I am out of here before you replace me with one of your look-alike robots."

With everyone's attention now clearly focused on Gabe's outburst, Alex gently eased her way to a doorway on the other side of the glass partition. Gabe spotted her out of the corner of his eye, but had no idea what she was up to or how he would be able to reach her without being stopped by one adult or another.

As luck would have it, the elevator door opened again, this time revealing Danielle Foster, accompanied by none other than Pete McDonough. As everyone's gaze shifted for what was no more than an instant, Gabe made a dash to the far end of the room as Alex pushed the door open.

Neither Gabe nor Alex had any idea where they were or where they were heading, but for the moment, they were out of the clutches of all three generations of Fosters. That was all that mattered. Once again without a plan, Gabe hoped that Alex had something up her sleeve. But from the look on her face, she seemed to be at as much of a loss for any ideas as he was. For now, they were simply propelled by the speed at which their feet could carry them the furthest possible distance from this underground experimental chamber.

They found themselves in a long, narrow corridor with no exit immediately in sight. Gabe knew that they had less than a minute's head start and simply had to keep going, no matter what. Any questions about who Julia and Rose were or how Uncle Bernie figured into all of this would have to wait.

The lighting dimmed to almost complete blackness as Gabe and Alex reached the end of the corridor that branched into several smaller underground tunnels. There was no way of knowing which, if any, might lead them to safety or whether they would just circle back to the waiting adults.

"I can barely see anything, Gabe. Which way should we go?" Alex asked, uncharacteristically unsure of herself.

"Oh great, you're asking me. I don't have a clue," Gabe answered. "But wait, stop for a second, do you hear anything?" he asked.

"No, what do you hear?" Alex asked.

"That's just it, I don't hear anything. Nobody is coming after us."

"Well, maybe they know there is no way out of here and they're just waiting for us to figure that out and head back to the lab," Alex guessed.

"Or maybe they just want us to think that so we'll give up," Gabe said trying not to be outsmarted by the adults.

"So do we just stay here or keep going?" Alex asked. For the first time, she relied on Gabe to take the next step.

"Well I may not be very book smart, but I do have a pretty good sense of direction and from what I can tell given the location of this building, the direct descent that the elevator made to the basement, and the location of the door we used to get into these tunnels, if we take this left turn and the tunnel goes far enough we should wind up somewhere under Central Park. If I'm wrong, then I hope you're a good swimmer because we'll be somewhere under the Hudson River. Well, park or river, that is just a risk we'll have to take," Gabe declared, suddenly taking control of the situation, much to Alex's relief.

The twosome stumbled along in the near darkness, nervously feeling their way along the tunnel's walls. With no one behind them, Gabe and Alex slowed their pace a bit, checking for possible air vents or other escape routes. With no one behind them, their fears subsided for the moment as they assumed that whoever had gone to the trouble to construct this underground maze had to have an exit strategy at the other end. With no one behind them, their confidence surged as they were convinced they had eluded the band of mad scientists, at least temporarily. With no one behind them, Gabe and Alex never anticipated colliding with the rather tall, somewhat hunched over figure in front of them.

Chapter Eighteen

The Great Escape

"Follow me," the soft, low-pitched gravelly voice uttered. "There's a long winding stone staircase about ten yards ahead. It will lead you to a small platform on which you'll find a narrow metal ladder. It won't hold you both at the same time. You'll have to climb up carefully, one at a time. It's a long and somewhat treacherous climb, but when you get to the top, you'll find an opening with a padlocked metal cover."

The man fumbled with his jacket for a moment, pulling something from his vest pocket. "Use this key to open the lock. It'll take some strength, but I think you'll be able to push the cover open, Gabe."

Gabe reached out to take the key, looking as closely as he could at the face that belonged to the voice. In the darkness, he could barely make out any of the man's features, but yet there was something uncannily familiar about the voice.

"Who are you and why are you helping us escape?" Gabe asked cautiously.

"There's really no time for questions, young man and the answers will all come in good time. For now, I suggest you take your young companion and follow my instructions," the stranger replied.

"One more thing, Gabe, before I send you on your way, do you still have the notebook you found in the airplane seat pocket, the one with the formulas that made no sense to you?" the man inquired. Gabe tried desperately to identify the voice.

"I think so," Gabe answered. "It's in my back pocket, but how did you know about the notebook or that it made no sense to me?"

"Good! No need to concern yourself with how I know what or when I knew it. Just make sure you hold onto the notebook no matter what. There is a small hand-drawn map on the next to last page. When you reach the surface, follow it into the park. It will take you to your destination. I'll meet you both there in two hours. I'd happily join you on your ascent to the surface, but doubt that I'd make it more than a few steps, not to mention how terribly I'd slow you youngsters down."

"Why are you helping us, if you are even helping us? How do we know you're not just leading us right back into the Fosters' hands with this twisted set of directions?" By this time, Gabe was not about to believe anything that any adult said to him.

"Exactly," Alex chimed in. "How do we know we can trust you? We don't even know who you are, how you know who we are, or what your connection is to the professor, or the other Fosters, or that Philip Kingsley creep for that matter," she exclaimed.

"You don't, my young friends, but at some point you're going to need to trust someone to get you out of this mess, and I suggest that I'm your best bet at the moment. The others will be after you shortly. I've just managed to slow them down, but I'm afraid they won't be stopped that easily." The man stepped back, tipping his baseball cap so that the Brooklyn Dodgers logo was just barely visible in the near darkness of the tunnel.

With that, he turned to leave, now quite clearly leaning on his cane as he slowly made his way through a previously hidden doorway into an adjacent passage. "I suggest you take your leave immediately, children. I will see you shortly." His voice trailed off in the distance and the sound of his cane preceded the slow labored steps of his walk.

"Alex, am I going crazy or something? That couldn't have been the guy from the SUV who was just about to pop my head open back there? Why would he be trying to help us escape? I don't get it."

"I don't get it either, Gabe. Was the old man in the lab the same one you met on the plane? Are there two Professor Fosters? Or are they the same person?"

"They sure looked the same from what I could see, and the voices sounded the same, but there was something different that I just can't put my finger on," Gabe wondered aloud.

"The baseball cap, that's it, the baseball cap!" Gabe exclaimed.

"What baseball cap? What are you talking about?" Alex asked.

"The old man on the plane was wearing a Brooklyn Dodgers baseball cap! The one back there in the lab wasn't."

"You're right, Gabe, the old guy in the SUV wasn't wearing a baseball cap," Alex replied. "Well, I guess he could've taken it off," Alex reasoned.

"He could have, but he didn't take it off, not even once on a five-hour flight from LA. And the notebook, this guy knew about the notebook. He had to be the old man from the plane," Gabe insisted. He was trying to make sense out of a situation that was making less sense with every passing minute.

"Let's get out of here while we can, Gabe," Alex urged. She grabbed Gabe's hand and pulled him in the direction of the promised stone staircase.

With hands outreached in the darkness, Gabe and Alex actually felt the stone steps before they saw them. They began their ascent, step by step, slipping from time to time on the uneven surface and stopping to catch their breath after what seemed like an endless climb. As he attempted to mount the next step, just ahead of Alex, Gabe's right foot came to rest next to his left. There were no more steps. They finally reached the platform.

The old man had been truthful, at least to this point, but Gabe could not help feeling skeptical about what was yet to come.

"Gabe, here's the ladder," Alex shouted, as if she had made some groundbreaking archaeological discovery.

"The ladder won't hold both of us at the same time," Gabe reminded Alex. I'll go first so that I can open the lock and lift the cover. That should give us some light and make it easier for you to find your way to the surface. Will you be okay down here? I have no idea how high this thing goes or how long it will take me to get to the top." He was genuinely concerned about leaving Alex at the bottom by herself.

"I'm good, Gabe," Alex reassured him. She knew that this was the only logical plan given that it was more likely that Gabe would have the needed strength to open the cover. "I've explored enough virtual dark caves and excavation sites on the internet and in my imagination to be able to handle this, I think," she said, with just the slightest hesitation and a little less bravado than usual.

"I'm heading up, Alex. Just keep talking. Say anything, sing a song if you have to. Just let me know you're okay down there," Gabe instructed, as he started his climb up the ladder. "I never remember the words to any songs, but I'm pretty good at humming so I'll just hum so we can keep track of each other, okay Alex?" Gabe said, as his voice trailed off up the ladder.

Gabe's humming became fainter and fainter, when he suddenly shouted in pain. "Ouch," he yelled, as he hit his head on the metal closure at the top of the ladder. "I've made it, Alex. I've just got to get this key into the lock. So far so good, it fits. The old man hasn't lied to us yet."

With the lock now open, Gabe attempted to push the cover off of the opening with one hand, but it wouldn't budge. He knew he would need the strength of both hands, but was afraid that if he let go of the ladder, he would lose his balance and fall who knows what distance. Gabe was not particularly fond of heights as his airplane experiences had proven, but fortunately in the dark, he had no real sense of just how high up he was. He loosened his grip on the ladder and pushed as hard as he could with both hands.

Along with the first stream of daylight he had seen in what seemed like forever, Gabe almost passed out at the sight of the distance between him and Alex some fifty feet below him on the platform. He crawled onto the surface and secured the ladder for Alex's ascent, looking around briefly to see where in the world, or at least in Manhattan, he was.

Alex arrived at the top of the ladder a few minutes later, cautiously climbing one step at a time. As she neared the surface, Gabe reached down to pull her to the sidewalk at Central Park West and 72nd Street, about one hundred feet from the impressive architectural structure known as The Dakota, home to the rich and famous.

Gabe and Alex stood up amid some surprised looks from pedestrians and motorists passing them on either side of what appeared to be an ordinary manhole cover. They brushed themselves off, and got their bearings as Gabe pulled the notebook from his back pocket.

He opened the notebook from the back, anxious to locate the map on the next to last page as the old man had directed him. There was no map, and as he anxiously turned to the first page, there were no formulas. The pages were empty. This was not the notebook he had found on the plane. Someone had switched it for this blank one.

Although free to head anywhere they chose in Manhattan, Gabe and Alex were no closer to understanding anything that had happened to them in the last several hours. They did not know who Julia was or just how much of a threat she posed to the professor. Gabe still had no idea just how Uncle Bernie figured into this. And most importantly, they did not know who the real Professor Foster was or if he had some diabolical plan to unleash a generation of robot children to replace the less than perfect Gabes in the world.

Chapter Nineteen

The Notebook

It turned out that no one had intentionally switched the notebooks. When Gabe reached into his backpack, half asleep in the wee hours of the morning before leaving Sag Harbor for Manhattan, he pulled his empty homework pad out instead of the notebook left behind on the plane by the professor. This was an honest, but a careless, and now somewhat costly mistake that left him and Alex without any particular plan.

At the same time, however, Gabe's dad finally had something to go on. He had no idea who the notebook belonged to or what any of the contents meant, but for the moment it was the only clue he had as to his son's scatter-brained adventure though Manhattan.

Martin had thrown Gabe's backpack containing his summer homework into the trunk of the Volvo that morning, hoping that he could get Gabe to do some reading if the time in the assistant district attorney's office dragged on. He had carried it up to the office suite, deposited it in the waiting area before his meeting with Alex's mom, and then picked it up again as they embarked on their search for the kids.

"I've been dragging this thing around with me all day, Penny. Maybe I should take a look inside to see if there is any clue as to what Gabe was planning to do or why he wanted to go to the Kingsley Institute," Martin said. He was hoping for any lead to go on. A half eaten sandwich, several snack bar wrappers, two clearly never opened books, a DVD player, iPad, and two sets of headphones later, Gabe's dad found a notebook with some odd looking writing; definitely not his son's.

"Don't these look like formulas or some sort of scientific notation to you, Penny?" Martin asked.

"I'm not much of a scientist, Marty, but it could be something that belonged to the professor. If Foster gave this to your son to hold onto for him, Gabe could be much more involved in this than either of us thought. I'm sure he has no idea what he's gotten himself into, chasing after this old guy, not to mention dragging Alex into this mess," Penny said. While her tone was almost sympathetic, she was no less anxious to get her hands on the notebook.

"Come to think of it, that notebook could be a useful piece of evidence. Don't handle it any more than you have to, Marty. The last thing we need is your fingerprints all over it. Let me get some gloves on and we'll take a closer look."

The assistant district attorney pulled a pair of disposable gloves from her purse, slipped them on and began to examine the notebook Martin had removed from Gabe's backpack. "Well the scientific writing means nothing to me, but I'm sure our lab geeks will find it interesting," Penny concluded.

"Let me just look. I won't touch," Gabe's dad promised. He looked on intently at the pages as Alex's mom flipped through them. "There is something there in the back. Look at the next to last page. It's some sort of a diagram or map," Martin said excitedly.

"There are some initials and abbreviations of street names leading from somewhere on the west side to the east side of C.P., which I would guess is Central Park," Gabe's dad said in an almost whisper as he examined the writing.

"And then it says… I'm not really sure if this is an I or an L. The next letter is a G. I'm pretty sure of that, I.G. or L.G, and then it ends at either I.G. or L.G. I have no clue what that might mean, I.G. or L.G.," Martin said. He turned to Penny, hoping for some clarity.

"We need some sort of map of Central Park to see if either of those sets of initials mean anything. But we also need to get a reading on these formulas. If any of them lead us to whatever it was that killed Leonard Harvey, that pretty much would seal the deal on linking the professor to his murder," she replied. Alex's mom once again struggled with whether her priority should be locating the kids or making her case against P.J. Foster.

Gabe's dad and Alex's mom agreed that there was no longer any point in heading to University Hospital. Whoever was lying in the burn unit there was neither of the children nor Professor Foster. Whichever Penny's priority, finding Gabe and Alex or arresting her prime suspect, it seemed as if their best bet was somewhere in Central Park.

Coincidence or not, Gabe had pretty much come to the same conclusion. If he was going to stay clear of the band of mad scientists back in the lab or be reunited with the real Professor Foster before his father, or heaven forbid his mother, got hold of him, he and Alex had better make their way into the park. They had to trust that something or someone would lead them to wherever it was that map was supposed to take them. At least they were above ground for now. With the park full of holiday visitors on this late afternoon in July, there would be enough people, particularly kids, around so that they could blend in without attracting too much attention.

"Well, I may be the planner, but you're the one with the sense of direction," Alex said.

"I know we're on the west side of the park. That awesome building is The Dakota. Believe it or not, Alex, that's where Philip Kingsley lives, or at least it's where my dad met with him last summer when he took me into the city with him for the meeting with that creep," Gabe replied.

"That means we're about eight blocks or so from the American Museum of Natural History," Alex added. "Just about anything any bona fide archaeologist in training could hope to see first-hand is in that museum."

"Maybe that's it. Isn't that the dinosaur museum?" Gabe asked. "If we started our underground journey somewhere around West 86th Street and wound up southeast of where we began, here in front of The Dakota, then it's very possible that when the second and I think real Professor Foster took that other underground passage, he could have been heading somewhere in the direction of the American Museum of Natural History," Gabe reasoned. He seemed to be exhibiting a new found logic that had escaped him in any effort he had ever made in or about school.

"Then that's clearly where we will not be going," Gabe continued. He now seemed to have discovered some inner confidence he had never experienced before.

"If the professor wanted us to join him there, he would have simply had us go along with him through that other passage. He doesn't want us there, if that's even where he went, at least not at this point. Wherever he needs us to be has to be somewhere in the park itself, somewhere out of the way of whatever he still needs to take care of back at the lab or possibly the museum."

"Wait a second, wait a second," Alex blurted. "You're right, but maybe for the wrong reasons. If the old man...I mean the real old man, the one from the tunnel, is on his way to the museum, it may have something to do with his famous archaeologist grandson, Jonas Foster. With everyone thinking Jonas Foster is dead, especially this Julia character, there may be something the professor needs to get his hands on before anyone else can from Jonas Foster's research which just happens to be archived at the..."

"Don't tell me," Gabe shouted. "The American Museum of Natural History."

"You got it!" Alex said gleefully.

The two agreed that their best strategy at the moment was to leave P.J. Foster to his work. They would somehow navigate their way to his previously directed, but for the moment unknown location, most likely somewhere in Central Park.

"Okay, let's head into the park and get hold of one of those tourist maps that lists all of the major sites. We're bound to figure something out," Gabe declared.

Chapter Twenty

The Imposter

As the old man navigated his way through the hidden doorway into the narrow tunnel and away from the children, he felt reassured knowing that Gabe and his young friend had escaped. For the moment, they were out of Philip Kingsley's clutches and free of the imposter Kingsley had inserted at the underground research facility. Apparently the switch had gone undetected by everyone, including his grandson Jonas and great granddaughter Danielle.

Kingsley had assured the professor that the impersonation was necessary to provide the needed cover for the scientist to continue his work in secret. "This is simply an innocent ruse so that you might complete the project without any interference from the press or needless intrusion by government officials," Kingsley had promised.

But this had not been just any imposter. This was about the best Kingsley could hope for if he was going to pull this off. This was the renowned Professor Foster's younger brother, Thaddeus Jedediah Foster. Three years P.J. Foster's junior, T. J. Foster, at age ninety-seven, had been living in a nursing home for the past ten years.

Phineas hadn't even known that his brother was still alive, having been in Europe and pretty much out of contact with everyone from his past for nearly thirty years. He had been stunned to learn that Kingsley knew of his brother's whereabouts and could summon him so easily. .

What Phineas hadn't known was that it was his own estranged daughter Julia who had sequestered Thaddeus away a decade ago, supposedly for his own good, but much more for hers. She knew that Uncle Thaddeus would serve her well when the right time came, and now indeed was the right time. The two brothers looked so much alike, particularly as they aged, that substituting one for the other had seemed like the most logical of plans to Kingsley. Oddly, the younger brother's existence came to Kingsley's attention quite by accident. At least that was what he had told Phineas.

"How fortuitous, my dear Professor Foster, that I should discover that your brother is still alive and residing in a nursing home in Connecticut, not more than seventy-five miles from the Institute," the professor recalled Kingsley saying.

"My goodness. I thought the old bugger was dead for sure," Phineas remembered answering.

"Well he's been in a bad way, no money and no family to look after him, but all of that has changed now. I've put him up in a hotel in the city, with a companion of course. He is just blocks away from where we are, and in short order I will see to it that you have a proper reunion. For now, permit me to enlist his assistance in concealing you from the public eye and we will all have much to celebrate when our work is done," Kingsley had explained.

Phineas was rather astounded that the imposter, despite the uncanny physical resemblance between him and his younger brother, had deceived both his grandson Jonas, and especially his great granddaughter Danielle. But he was much relieved at the reappearance of the man who had practically been a son to him, Bernard Marshall. Bernard would not be fooled as the others were. The professor was convinced of that.

There was so much more of what had happened to the old man in the last two days that Gabe did not yet know. And it was these events that flashed through the professor's mind as he returned to the museum to retrieve his files.

He had been delivered from JFK to the Kingsley Institute by taxi as planned just over thirty-six hours ago. Kingsley's staff had taken great pains to replicate every last detail of his wardrobe in order to make the switch between brothers believable. With no hope of locating another authentic Brooklyn Dodgers baseball cap, Kingsley had pleaded with the professor to relinquish his treasured souvenir in order to complete the disguise. But there was no possible way he would part with one of the two caps he had bought at the last game played in Ebbets Field on September 24, 1957. The matching cap was equally treasured by its owner, Bernard Marshall, and although not worn on a daily basis, was stored securely in Uncle Bernie's Brooklyn apartment.

The evening that the professor spent with Kingsley at the Institute had been fairly unremarkable. Aside from dinner and a discussion of the plan to move the operation to the West 86th Street underground facility the next morning, most of it had been devoted to obtaining the necessary information to brief Foster's double.

Kingsley had insisted that the two brothers not meet just yet. He had allowed for a videoconference hookup between the Institute and the younger brother's hotel suite in order to ensure that the low muffled voice pattern, and slow and deliberate walk were a match. Then there were some facts and people's names and faces the professor's brother would have to master before dawn, but the gentleman had been a fast learner despite his advanced age. Kingsley had been quite confident that this would come off without a hitch despite the professor's doubts.

The switch had been made the next morning when the imposter left his hotel with Kingsley's driver. Kingsley had arranged for them to meet Danielle who joined her would-be great grandfather in the Black Escalade. All had gone according to plan until the blaze broke out in the first floor kitchen of the upper Westside brownstone. The flames had spread so rapidly to the upper floors that there was no doubt that some accelerant had been used. There was no question that the fire had been set deliberately.

The professor had just awakened and assisted by one of Kingsley's staff was dressing in the first floor guest bedroom when the smoke alarms sounded. Instinctively, the young man had grabbed P.J. Foster as he reached for his cap and cane, and had pulled him out through a patio door to a back garden. Together the two made their way through the garden to an alley that led to the street. There they had hailed a cab as the blaze intensified and the sirens blared, announcing the arrival of the NYFD.

"Another of that man's promises. So far they've led to kidnap, murder, and our near incineration," Phineas remembered saying, as the young staff member literally had dragged him away from the flames consuming the Institute.

Indeed, Kingsley had made one promise after another, and then broken each one in turn. But that was before he lay in University Hospital recovering from second and third degree burns, an unfortunate occurrence, but one that might finally release the professor from Kingsley's grasp.

"I'm not sure where I'm supposed to take you Professor Foster, but I had to get you out of there immediately," the young man had declared.

"Good thinking, my boy. We need not go very far. Have the driver make his way to the American Museum of Natural History, just a few blocks from here, if I recall correctly. Not the main entrance, but the small employees' entrance on the south side of the building. My grandson Jonas has an office there that is connected through a series of underground passageways to our much larger research facility on West 86th Street."

"My files are secured in his office and I will need access to them in order to continue with the project once I am reunited with my young acquaintance Gabriel. Your employer asked me to move the files to the Institute when I arrived yesterday. Good for him and especially me that I did no such thing. They would be reduced to ashes by now if I did not follow my own instincts," the professor concluded.

The taxi had stopped at the traffic light on Central Park West at the corner of 79th Street, signaling a left turn when the professor turned to the young man. "The question for me now is what do my instincts tell me about you, young man? Should I trust you, young fellow? You acted without hesitation back there and probably saved both of our lives."

"More importantly, Professor Foster, I do know a bit about what Dr. Kingsley was planning next, once he was certain that all of the key players were in place in the lab and ready to take their final orders from the one and only Professor P.J. Foster. I do know he had very little regard for the actual outcome of your research and even less concern about the wellbeing of Gabriel Marx," the young man had explained.

"Then what was he up to, young man?" the professor had inquired.

"Dr. Kingsley wanted to use your work to create a prototype, a mechanism for programming young people, a way to insure global political and financial influence for NIBS, to be made available to the highest bidder. He understood the mind control piece. But he had to convince everyone that his project would somehow benefit young people. He had to conceal his sinister motives. And that's why he needed you."

The conversation had been interrupted by the taxi's sudden stop at their destination. The twosome had exited the cab and made their way to a set of stone steps leading down to the basement of the museum. Once inside, the young man whose name was still unknown to the professor had helped the old man to a chair where he had been able to observe a series of monitors. The surveillance system was quite sophisticated and revealed the movements within the passageways leading to the underground lab. Phineas instantly had spotted Gabe and the young girl who accompanied him, as they ran with great urgency from the direction of the lab. At the sight of the two children, Phineas had bolted from his seat so suddenly that his companion thought the old man had taken ill.

"Where are you going, Professor Foster? Are you all right?" the young man had asked.

"Not very far, my boy. Just far enough to retrieve those youngsters before my years of work are completely corrupted. It is now quite clear that I wasn't sequestered at the Institute for my own good," the professor had added.

"No indeed, sir, you were to be kept out of the way just long enough for my father to execute his plan, no matter what harm would come to young Gabriel Marx or your reputation."

"Your father? My reputation? Philip Kingsley is your father?" the professor had said incredulously. "Why have you come to my rescue then, young man? What do you gain by helping me? And why have you revealed so much to me?"

The young Kingsley had begun to answer when the professor brushed past him on his mission to get to the children. "Never mind. I have no time to waste right now. Wait here until I return. I'm probably crazy to trust anyone named Kingsley at this point, but what choice do I have?"

Chapter Twenty-One

A Familiar Face in an Unfamiliar Place

Gabe and Alex made their way through the park, passing ice cream, hotdog, and souvenir vendors along the way. Dozens of children were lined up for a turn to order their favorite flavors while others clutched balloons and showed off their freshly painted butterfly, tiger, and superhero faces.

"I'm starving. Do you have any money, Alex? We haven't eaten anything in hours and we've got to get hold of one of those maps. This place is huge and there is no way we're going to figure out where the professor wanted us to meet him without something or someone to help us." Gabe was beginning to feel more discouraged than he cared to admit.

Alex reached into her various pockets, but came up empty handed, except for some odd-looking hair clip she didn't remember she had. "Whatever I had was in my backpack, and I left that behind when we made a run for it," she answered. "I hate to admit it, Gabe, but I am out of ideas for the moment."

"We can't give up now. Let's just keep walking. We're bound to figure something out as long as no one is breathing down our necks," Gabe said.

"Or trying to unscramble and reprogram your brain," Alex added, remembering just why they made a run for it in the first place.

"Well, we may have just lucked out," Alex blurted out. "We may have to put up with our growling stomachs for a while longer, but there's one of those directory maps posted on that bulletin board over there." She grabbed Gabe by the hand and pulled him toward the display of the park's major sites that stood just to the right of the path on which they were walking.

With the large display in front of them, Gabe was once again reminded that even with the map, he might not be much use. There were landmarks and park attractions listed all over, most of which he could hardly read. He had a good sense of direction and was great at finding places by instinct, but reading and interpreting a map was a totally different challenge, and one he was too embarrassed to confess to Alex that he couldn't handle.

"Remember Alex, I can't read without my glasses," Gabe said, again relying on his tried and true excuse.

"I'm not tall enough to reach the top. Give me a boost, Gabe," Alex replied.

Gabe bent down and cupped his hands as Alex stepped up to reach the highest section of the map. She held on tightly to Gabe's shoulders as they both did their best to keep their balance.

"There are a whole bunch of places listed here. How are we supposed to know which one the professor meant? There are fountains, monuments, theaters. There's a reservoir, a zoo, a boathouse. There's even some medieval looking castle." Alex climbed to a fully seated position across Gabe's shoulders to get a better view. Gabe staggered under her weight for a moment, but managed to regain his equilibrium and steady himself.

"Wow, you two are quite a circus act," the familiar voice declared, startling both of them as the soft grass broke their fall. Gabe and Alex looked up into the early evening sunset. Blinded by the glare, it took them a moment to realize they were glancing up at none other than their original fellow sleuth, Pete McDonough.

Pete stretched out both of his arms, pulling Gabe and Alex to their feet. "So I finally caught up with the two of you. You've pulled off a couple of really cool escapes today, but I gave your dad my word, Gabe, that I wouldn't lose sight of you again. With the exception of a few hairy moments back there, I didn't break my promise to Mr. M. He's in quite a state over the two of you. He's racing around the city with your mom Alex, who's got half of the NYPD looking for you, not to mention your mom Gabe, who from your dad's voicemails and texts sounds like the FBI and CIA rolled into one."

"How did you find us?" Gabe asked, worried about who else might show up.

"There was quite a commotion at that underground lab when the two of you took off. Did you get a look at how many Gabes there were behind that glass partition? Quite frankly, that place gave me the creeps, and I took my cue from you guys and got out while the getting was good," Pete answered.

"I pretty much left the way I came in, although your exit was much more dramatic," Pete continued. Danielle had the code for the elevator and up we went... me,

Danielle, and someone named Bernard who said he is your uncle. We just left while everyone else was running around in circles trying to figure out how the two of you got out," Pete explained.

"But how did you find us?" Gabe repeated.

"For that, my friends, I give all the credit to Danielle Foster. Apparently she managed to plant a tracking device in one of your pockets when you first got into the Escalade after she located you at the fire. We lost you for some time there. Danielle knew you were in some underground passageway and figured we'd pick up your signal as soon as you surfaced," Pete continued.

Alex reached into her back pocket and retrieved what moments ago she thought was an unfamiliar hair clip. "Do you mean this thing?" she asked, examining it more closely for signs of life. Before either Gabe or Pete could stop her, she threw the device into a nearby wooded area with all the force she could muster.

"Now what did you go and do that for, Alex? How are we going to hook up with Danielle and Gabe's uncle?" Pete asked, clearly exasperated.

"That's just it. We're not!" Alex insisted.

"We're not?" Gabe asked and then repeated with some newly discovered confidence, "We're not!"

"That old guy back there in the lab is an imposter. We don't know who he is, but he is not the real P.J. Foster. At least he is not the one I met on the plane yesterday," Gabe declared.

"Hold on, hold on guys," Pete interrupted. "I wouldn't know one P.J. Foster from another, but Uncle Bernie figured that out pretty quickly. That's why he took off with Danielle and me," Pete explained. "He seemed very worried about the real professor's safety once he realized there had been a switch. This Uncle

Bernie guy knew even more about the underground tunnels than Danielle. He knew that they led to more than one place, and was pretty sure you would make your way to the park. He figured if I could catch up with you, he and Danielle would try to find the professor."

"Okay, so we all agree on two things, someone is impersonating the actual P.J. Foster and the real professor is probably in grave danger, not to mention that he is on the verge of being arrested for murder. But that doesn't mean we can just stand around here," Alex interjected. "We've got to figure out where he wanted us to meet him and unless you have something else to tell us, we have about thirty minutes left until the two hours are up that he gave us," Gabe explained.

While Gabe and Alex had seen the real professor a little more than an hour ago, they had no idea where he was at that moment. They could only hope that Uncle Bernie and Danielle knew enough about the tunnels leading away from the lab to find him. More importantly, they knew they had to get to him before their parents, the NYPD, and whoever was behind the scheme to make the switch got their hands on the professor.

Pete had been pretty helpful to them earlier that day. Just maybe, if they all worked together, they could figure something out. "Pete, put the phone away and stay focused," Alex insisted.

"But I have something else to tell you, and you're not gonna be too happy about this news either," Pete replied, looking down at his cell phone. "Your dad just texted me, Gabe. He's just arrived in the park with your mom, Alex, and big as this place is, I get the feeling that we're all in for one big family gathering before the night is out."

Chapter Twenty-Two

All Roads Lead to Central Park

Gabe's dad and Alex's mom, with their combined years of legal expertise, investigative skill, and parental anxiety, were now certain that the children were heading for some location in Central Park. I.G. or L.G., whatever that stood for, that's where they were going.

"Take a look. I've got some information about the park on my iPad," Penny said as the squad car made its way across town. "I don't see anything that even remotely fits those initials. The only thing I can think of is that the G could stand for gate."

"There are quite a few of those, but they're just entrances to the park, Merchant's Gate, Engineer's Gate, Artist's Gate, but nothing with L.G. for sure," she mumbled as she scrolled down the computer screen.

"Let me see; maybe you're missing something," Martin insisted.

He stared at the screen for several seconds, muttering under his breath. "It's not L.G. Wait a minute, here it is. It's I.G. and it must stand for Inventor's Gate," he shouted, unable to contain his excitement. "That's it, Inventor's Gate, 72nd Street and Fifth Avenue, smack in the heart of Manhattan. That's the entrance to the park that the map was referring to," he concluded.

"Of course, that makes sense," Penny responded.

She instructed the police officer at the wheel of the squad car to move the vehicle from the southernmost entrance of the park near 59th Street east to Madison Avenue and up to 72nd Street.

"Wouldn't we be better off on foot at this point? The last thing we need to do is come charging into Central Park like the cavalry," Martin cautioned when they reached the corner of 72nd Street and Madison Avenue.

"Good point. Pull over and we'll walk the rest of the way," Penny told the officer.

The two parents exited the car. Martin stopped for a moment as they approached the park, just long enough to send a brief text to Pete as to their whereabouts.

"Do you really think that's a good idea?" Penny asked.

"Look, we know that this Inventor's Gate location has some significance, but we still don't know what that is. The last communication from Pete indicated that he had spotted the kids somewhere on the west side of the park. We have no idea if they're still there, on their way here, or who knows where else by now. Between Pete and this map, we just may be able to finally find them," Martin argued.

They approached the park entrance cautiously, rotating their glance from one side of the street to the other to be certain not to miss the children among the tourists and bystanders. Plainly carved into the stone entrance to the park at 72nd Street were the words Inventor's Gate.

"This is it. Do you see them, Marty?" Penny asked hopefully.

"Not yet," Martin answered. "But we just can't stand here waiting for them as if we had a pre-arranged appointment. We're completely conspicuous, and if they spot us, which they surely will, they're bound to head off in another direction."

"Well, you could try hiding behind a tree or getting your face painted at the Children's Zoo." Martin was startled by the all too familiar voice. He was certain that his heart had momentarily stopped at the shock of Gabe's mother's appearance from behind. And while stunned to see Elly Marshall in the middle of Central Park, he was equally surprised to see her accompanied by her octogenarian Uncle Bernie. But what startled Martin and Penny even more was the young woman referred to as Danielle when the introductions began.

The five of them awkwardly exchanged greetings as Martin said, "Penny, this is Gabe's mother Elly and her uncle, Bernie Marshall."

"And this is Danielle Foster, the professor's great granddaughter," Uncle Bernie interrupted.

Now it was Penny's turn to have her heart stop briefly as she heard the name Foster.

"If we can dispense with all of the formalities, what exactly is going on here and how did you know about this place, Elly? I know you said something about Uncle Bernie on the phone earlier, but I figured that was just your imagination running away with itself for a change," Martin said.

"It is not her imagination at all," Uncle Bernie interjected. "I am rather well acquainted with your prime murder suspect, Ms. Cooper, and I can assure you that you are after the wrong man."

"That remains to be seen, Mr. Marshall, doesn't it? But since you claim to be so knowledgeable about my murder suspect, please enlighten us all," Penny requested. She tried to remain polite, but was becoming increasingly agitated at the growing number of people all standing around while her daughter and the most wanted man in New York City were still at large.

"And Danielle Foster, is it, the professor's great granddaughter? No doubt you can provide an alibi which will clear P.J. Foster of all suspicion?" Penny continued, unable to conceal the sarcasm in her voice.

"Not an alibi, Ms. Cooper, but most certainly an explanation," Danielle responded.

"Before we consider alibis or explanations from either of you, why don't you just tell me where the professor is and if the children are with him," Penny demanded.

The mounting tension among the old and new acquaintances was broken by the signal of an incoming text on Martin's phone. "It's from Pete."

With Gabe and Alex near lake in front of fountain. Where r u? Gabe's dad read the message aloud.

"They're at Bethesda Fountain." Penny exclaimed. "Let's go!"

"They are not at Bethesda Fountain," Danielle interrupted. "I planted a tracking device in Alex's pocket. They're still near the entrance on the west side of the park. Gabe and Alex continue doing their best to outsmart us and now it seems that they've managed to get Pete to go along with them again for some reason."

"Tracking device? What are you, Ms. Foster; FBI, secret agent, or just your plain old everyday spy?" Martin asked.

"It's a long story, Mr. Marx, but trust me, the kids are not waiting for you at Bethesda Fountain," Danielle assured him.

"What next? Do we wait here or make our way to the other side of the park?" Elly asked, looking at Uncle Bernie for some direction.

"Neither," Uncle Bernie insisted, as he spotted the approaching wheelchair and the Brooklyn Dodgers baseball cap atop the head of its occupant. "You wanted the professor and now you have him, Ms. Cooper. But let me assure you, he is not the murderer," Uncle Bernie declared.

"I'll be the judge of that, but not until we know the children are safe," Penny replied.

Indeed, that was the big question, for even the professor had not seen Gabe and Alex for more than an hour, and could only hope that they would eventually make their way to this location.

"Do you know where Gabe and Alex are?" Uncle Bernie asked, now face to face with the real P.J. Foster.

"I wish I could say with certainty that I do, but if they followed my instructions and the directions in the notebook, they would have joined us by now," the professor answered.

And then the chorus of questions flew at the old man from every direction, as each voice grew louder and more demanding than the other.

"Why this location?"

"Where were they an hour ago?"

"What were you planning to do to my son?" Gabe's mom and dad fired one after the other.

"Why are we waiting here when I'm telling you they're on the west side of the park?" Danielle insisted.

"It seems we are getting nowhere with these questions," Martin finally concluded.

"Indeed, my good man," the professor responded. "I have every faith in Gabe and Alex to make their way back to us safely, but perhaps not just yet, as there may be more urgent matters to which they must attend."

Chapter Twenty-Three

False Alarm

Immediately following the text alerting Pete that Martin and company had arrived in Central Park, in hot pursuit of the missing Gabe and Alex, a second message appeared on the screen. *"Meet me at the fountain across from the boathouse. D.,"* Pete read aloud to his two young companions.

"Okay guys, it looks like we have our marching orders from the professor's great granddaughter," Pete announced. "Danielle obviously must have a line on the real Professor's whereabouts. Let's figure out where this place is and get ourselves over there before there are any more impostors to deal with," Pete continued.

"Exactly!" Gabe declared. "But what makes you think that Danielle knows where the real P.J. Foster is or that the text you just got even came from her?" Gabe asked.

Alex chimed in at that point. She nodded her head in obvious agreement with Gabe's skepticism about the source of the message. Pete seemed a bit thrown. He had to admit that given the twists and turns of the last few hours, it would be best to leave no stone unturned.

"You guys have a point. Let me check." Pete looked at the caller ID on his phone, and acknowledged that he did not recognize the previous incoming phone number.

"It seems you two have out sleuthed me on this one. It was a pretty stupid assumption on my part and a really good catch on your part," Pete admitted.

"So now what?" he added. Gabe and Alex looked to each other for some inspiration. They were tired, hungry and pretty much stumped when Gabe caught sight of one of the park's famous horse-drawn carriages, its driver decked out in top hat and tails.

Within moments the threesome was on board. As good as Gabe's sense of direction was, he realized there was no point trying to figure out how to get to the boathouse or the nearby fountain. Why keep going around in circles when they could be in the company of a most knowledgeable tour guide who could get them to their destination. What's more, this would give them a chance to rest their very weary bodies for a few moments.

Fortunately, Pete had a bit of cash on hand to pay the driver. Despite the steep fifty-dollar charge, they were on their way to Bethesda Fountain, no matter who it was who had summoned them there. At least they were aware that this was probably a trap to regain control of Gabe and proceed with who knows what sort of computer cloning experiment on him.

Pete was the first to disembark from the carriage that had stopped in front of the staircase leading down to the majestic statue of the angel Bethesda. As daylight began to fade, the few remaining rowboats on the lake made their way back to the boathouse across from where the statue stood. Gabe followed Pete and offered his hand to Alex to help her down. The terrace surrounding the statue was full of visitors snapping photos and insuring the fate of their wishes with the coins they tossed into the water.

In fact, nothing seemed out of the ordinary. Danielle was nowhere to be seen, which was no surprise, but neither were any of the other characters that Gabe and Alex had escaped from earlier.

"I'm not at all sure who or what we're looking for," Pete declared, and Gabe and Alex agreed.

"Should we split up?" Alex asked. "If they're looking for a young adult male and two kids, we're a pretty easy mark," she added.

"But if we head off in different directions, you guys are awfully vulnerable. Since you thought better of holding on to the tracking device Danielle planted on you, Alex, looking for you would be just about as easy as fining a needle in a haystack," Pete warned.

"We stay together!" Gabe insisted, taking charge. "There's strength in numbers or something like that. I'm just not sure if we should hang around up here and wait, or scout out the place to see if anyone or anything leads us to the real P.J. Foster."

With daylight just about completely gone, Gabe and company were grateful for the full moon and the star-filled summer sky. They began to descend the staircase to the fountain when Gabe spotted a lone rowboat floating in place near the water's edge. Some low hanging branches and the shadow cast by the moonlit night temporarily hid it.

Gabe was not the only one who caught sight of the seemingly passengerless rowboat as it emerged from behind the shadow of the brush that concealed it up until now. A police officer took off his shoes and socks, rolled up his pants legs and began wading out the several feet to reach the boat. The sightseers who just minutes ago casually strolled and sat along the terrace gathered to see what was happening.

Two other officers who had obviously been radioed for backup quickly exited their patrol car, lights flashing, as it pulled up to the curb near the staircase. A bomb squad vehicle approached from the other direction. The calm of the warm summer evening shifted in an instant to the alarm of a crowd that suddenly felt threatened, but by what?

At that moment, Pete made a decision he knew would not please Gabe and Alex. He texted their whereabouts to Gabe's dad. In the brief time that it took him to find the number and deliver the message, Gabe and Alex were gone. They had been standing no more than five feet from Pete as he turned for a moment to capture the light he needed to type his message. *With Gabe and Alex near lake in front of fountain. Where r u?*

Gabe and Alex had managed to elude Pete for the third time today, but not on their own this time, and not voluntarily. A uniformed Parks Department employee who insisted that they move away immediately because of the likely danger of an explosion separated them from Pete.

Pushed back into the crowd under the stone archway that lead away from Bethesda Fountain, they came upon an older woman. Gabe was startled to hear her call out his name. But when he heard the harsh tone of her voice, there was no need for a formal introduction. It took Gabe a moment, but he was certain he was face to face with none other than Julia. He and Alex were undoubtedly in the presence of Danielle Foster's grandmother, Jonas Foster's mother, and most importantly, Phineas Foster's estranged daughter.

The bomb scare turned out to be a false alarm. The contents of the rowboat looked pretty threatening at first. Shouts of, "It's a bomb; get down; clear the perimeter!" were heard from all directions. But when the men in hazmat suits concluded their work, it was determined to be a very real looking, absolutely harmless decoy. It had been located strategically to create the chaos Julia Foster needed to recapture Gabe and his friend.

Chapter Twenty-Four

Hear No Evil, See No Evil, Speak No Evil

With the appearance of Julia Foster, all four generations of Fosters were finally revealed to Gabe and Alex. But that was not the most interesting revelation to come as evening turned to night in the middle of Central Park, less than forty-eight hours since Gabe's arrival in New York. Julia, who was amazingly fit for someone in her mid seventies, was not about to try to detain the two almost teenagers by herself. She was accompanied by one of the lab assistants Gabe and Alex had managed to get away from earlier, as well as someone Julia repeatedly addressed as Philip.

This couldn't be the notorious Dr. Philip Kingsley, Gabe thought. There was a resemblance, but this seemed to be a younger and much more appealing version of the scientist who Gabe remembered from last summer.

"I trust you will not give us any more trouble than you already have," Julia said. "If you cooperate we will be finished in short order and certainly, Gabe, you will be the better for it, although that is of no particular consequence to me."

"Where are you taking us?" Alex interjected.

"Feisty little child you are, young lady. I'm not even sure how you got involved in this to begin with, but I doubt that you are in any position to be asking questions my dear," Julia replied rather brusquely.

While Gabe did not know where or how all of this would end, he was now quite convinced that he had met the mastermind of this whole scheme. Julia was as diabolical as everyone had described and presented much more of a challenge than anything he had confronted so far.

What he did not know was that Philip Jr. was no longer a collaborator of Julia's, or of Philip Sr.'s for that matter. Gabe was unaware of Philip Jr.'s earlier rescue of the professor from the fire. Gabe did not know that Philip Jr. had escorted the real P.J. Foster to the American Museum of Natural History, and waited patiently for the professor to navigate the underground passageway to locate the children once he had seen them on the surveillance cameras.

When P.J. Foster had returned to the museum, somewhat breathless, but otherwise remarkably energy-ized, Philip Jr. had confided whatever he knew of Julia's and his father's plan to destroy the old man. It was time to tell the professor the whole story.

He had explained that no one had actually murdered Leonard Harvey. Harvey had taken his own life because of Philip Kingsley's threats to reveal evidence that would have sent him to prison for decades on charges of fraud and embezzlement, despite the defense being prepared by his attorneys.

Harvey's suicide became a convenient way to implicate P.J. Foster as a murder suspect, place him at the mercy of Philip Kingsley and give Julia just the ammunition she needed to destroy her father once and for all.

For Dr. Philip Kingsley, the motive had always been power and greed. With this final phase of experimentation on his assortment of robotic Gabe clones, he would secure his preeminence and his fortune. For Julia it had been much more personal. She would finally see her father ruined. He would live out his remaining days as a convicted murderer, his own research completely distorted at the hands of Philip Kingsley.

Although Julia hadn't known what her father's secret files contained, she was certain that they did not include the brain-reprogramming scheme that Kingsley had devised. But that was of little consequence now. She was about to achieve her ultimate goal.

Philip Jr. was never a willing accomplice in his father's conspiracy. The controlling abusive patriarch gave him little choice. That is until he finally met the soft-spoken P.J. Foster a day earlier. He was not quite sure, but knew he was in the presence of a very different sort of man, one he could trust, one who would finally allow him to break the hold his father had on him. That was indeed the effect that P.J. Foster had on all the young people who crossed his path, all except his own daughter, whose jealousy blinded her to her father's gift.

Young Kingsley had been puzzled by most of the instructions the professor had given him upon his return from the underground passage to the museum, but knew better than to question the old man.

"Let me go with you, Professor Foster. You're in no shape to handle this on your own," he had pleaded.

"No, my boy, you are needed elsewhere if we are to put a stop to this. Get a wheelchair from the visitor's entrance to the museum. I'm afraid I can't do much more walking. Contact my grandson Jonas at this number. Put me and the chair into a taxi and leave the rest to me," the professor had insisted.

Once Philip Jr. had been certain that the professor was safely on his way to the Inventor's Gate on the east side of the park, accompanied by his grandson Jonas, he returned to the site of the devastating fire which almost completely consumed the Kingsley Institute. There he learned that his father had been rushed to the burn unit of University Hospital.

Convinced that Philip Sr. could do no more harm from his hospital bed and feeling little remorse at his father's critical condition, Philip Jr. had taken advantage of the trust Julia had placed in him and went along with her plan to retrieve Gabe and Alex.

Gabe stood fast as Philip Jr. took his arm and tried to lead him back up the steps to the tree-lined mall above. "Let go of me," Gabe said, trying to free himself from Philip Jr.'s grasp. He thought of screaming but realized that his protests would hardly be noticed with everyone still preoccupied with the commotion on the lake. He looked around frantically to see if he could catch sight of Pete, but saw no one he recognized. The other man led Alex up the staircase with Julia leading the way in front of both pairs.

Philip Jr. knew he had to give Gabe some sort of signal as soon as possible or risk his making a run for it. If Gabe tried to escape again, there was no telling what danger he might find himself in without Philip to safeguard him.

"Do you still have the key the professor gave you in the underground passageway?" he whispered. Gabe was stunned, knowing that only he, Alex and the real P.J.

Foster knew about the key and the planned meeting, whose time had long since passed.

"Just make it look like you're fighting me off and listen," he continued. "I'm here to help you, but I can't say anymore now."

Gabe was utterly thrown and unable to make eye contact with Alex, as she walked ahead of him. He so much wanted to rely on her for their next move, but had only his own judgment to count on. His instincts had served him well so far, but could he trust them yet again? With few options available to him, he had no choice in the matter. He continued to struggle with his unlikely new ally and did a very good job of making it look real.

"I'm texting the driver," Philip Jr. announced to Julia. "I'll have him pick us up at the west side of the park. Can you walk that far, Julia?" he added.

"No need to worry about my stamina, young man. Just don't let go of these two," Julia answered.

Philip Jr. did indeed send a text, but not to the driver. Rather he retrieved Pete's number from the previous text he sent, supposedly from Danielle, and sent off another. *U don't know me. Pls trust me. Kids r safe. Town Car PZK LAB at W 72nd St. Key in ignition.*

Chapter Twenty-Five

Rebel with a Cause

Pete had scarcely regained his footing after being jostled back and forth in the crowd as he searched desperately for a sighting of Gabe or Alex along the terrace surrounding Bethesda Fountain. He had no idea how he would possibly explain losing them for a third time in one day. He was not only accountable to Gabe's father at this point. He had to convince Danielle that he wasn't a total screw up as well.

The first text was from Danielle Foster. *r u on the west side of the park?*

Pete answered immediately. *NO!*

But before Danielle could respond, there was another message, not from Danielle, but from the number that had directed them to Bethesda Fountain in the first place. *U don't know me. Pls trust me. Kids r safe. Town Car PZK LAB at W 72nd St. entrance. Key in ignition.*

It was at that moment that Pete McDonough faced the biggest dilemma of his twenty-four years. There was no reason on earth to trust this message, given the events of the last hour. He didn't know who the message was from, if the sender actually had the kids, or where they were being taken.

The ringtone startled Pete so that he almost dropped the phone in the fountain as he pounced on the key to answer it. The call was from Martin, but it was not Martin's voice he heard when he answered.

"Peter, where are you?" the somewhat muffled voice uttered. "It's Danielle's great grandfather, Phineas."

Pete revealed his location, admitted Gabe's and Alex's most recent disappearance, and asked if he could trust the text he had just received. The answer from the old man was brief and clear, "Yes!"

The gathering at the Inventor's Gate had grown considerably since Gabe's dad and Alex's mom arrived. Joined now by Gabe's mother, Uncle Bernie, and most recently and to everyone's astonishment, P.J. Foster and his grandson, Jonas, this was indeed quite a reunion.

Gabe and Alex, on the other hand were in a Lincoln Town Car with Julia Foster, Philip Kingsley Jr., some lab assistant, and the driver.

"Where are you taking us?" Gabe asked. He was still not completely convinced that his handler was to be believed. Now with a better view of Alex who was rather agitated at this latest development, he tried to give her some reassurance that things were not as bad as they seemed.

When Gabe and Alex suddenly realized who was in the driver's seat, it took them both all the self-control they had not to call out to Pete as he sat with his hands on the steering wheel, decked out in chauffeur's cap and dark glasses. Despite Julia's determination to walk the distance to the car, she was just slow enough to give Pete the lead-time he needed to get there ahead of them as the text had instructed him.

Imagine Julia's surprise when rather than heading the several blocks uptown to the West 86th Street subterranean lab, the car turned south abruptly.

"What are you doing, driver? Turn this car around immediately!" she ordered. "Philip, stop him! What in heavens is going on here?"

Philip Jr. offered few words to the panicked architect of the plan to destroy P.J. Foster. "It's over, Julia. Whether Father survives his injuries or not, it's over," Philip pronounced. And for the second time today, Philip Jr. staked his position in direct opposition to his father.

Gabe and Alex looked at each other with the first bit of relief they had felt since arriving at the Kingsley Institute fire only twelve hours earlier. They didn't know exactly where they were being taken or who was waiting for them, but with Philip Jr. seated between them and Pete McDonough in the driver's seat, they were confident that this was about to come to a happy conclusion.

The car entered the park at West 65th Street where it traveled east across Fifth Avenue to Madison, uptown to 72nd Street and the waiting assembly of Fosters, Marshalls, Penny Cooper, and Martin Marx. Gabe, who had hoped for a ride from the airport in a limo the day before, was delighted with Pete's new vehicle.

"Nice wheels, Pete. Did Dad give you a promotion or something?" Gabe joked.

"No, but I think I may have a job working for the new director of the Kingsley Institute when all of this is over," he answered, glancing at Philip Jr. and Julia's increasingly reddening face in the rear view mirror.

When the car approached its destination, an array of police vehicles surrounded it. As Gabe opened the door, he was greeted by both his parents' embrace and not one question about whether or not he had done his summer reading. Remarkable indeed, what a little panic about their missing son had done to temper their concern about his schoolwork.

Alex ran to her mom, who started to admonish her, but quickly lapsed into hugs and tears. Danielle and her father put their arms around each other, still somewhat baffled by all that had unfolded in the last few hours. Philip Jr. stood alongside Pete, as they congratulated each other on an amazingly orchestrated partnership for two people who didn't know each other an hour ago.

"Do you kids have any idea what you pulled off today?" Penny Cooper asked. "We were completely wrong about the evidence and had drawn all of the wrong conclusions," she added.

"Up until about an hour ago, I was convinced that this was just another of your scatter-brained schemes, another ridiculous misadventure of yours, Gabe," Martin confessed. "If it wasn't for your determination and persistence, there is no telling how this all could have ended."

Gabe glanced at Alex, somewhat embarrassed by all of the praise, something he was not accustomed to getting from anyone, let alone his father.

"This kid of yours has what it takes, Mr. M., and Alex, you can be on my team any day of the week," Pete declared.

"I certainly would second that notion," Danielle agreed.

"These are indeed very exceptional young people to whom I owe a debt of gratitude for saving my grandfather's life as well as his reputation," Jonas Foster concluded. "Had they not had the courage and sheer nerve they displayed today, grandfather's work would have been completely corrupted by an experimental procedure that totally contradicted his intended mission," he added, looking directly at his obviously defeated mother.

Two police officers placed Julia in handcuffs, despite her protests of innocence, misunderstanding, and downright injustice. She was utterly flabbergasted by how this could have all gone so wrong after fifty years of meticulous and repeated plotting to ruin her father, and in turn punish Bernard Marshall.

As for P.J. Foster, he sat up a bit straighter in his wheelchair, but not at all in a celebratory way. This was an occasion that brought a mixture of emotions. He was reunited with his protégé Bernard whom he loved like a son, but who also reminded him of the tragic loss of the daughter he could not save. This pain was all the more agonizing as he confronted his surviving daughter whose vengeance could have destroyed everything he had worked for all of his life.

The professor made a simple request as Julia was taken into custody and the others planned to return to the comparative calm of their usual lives. "I would like to invite Gabe and Alex to join me and Bernard, not in my lab, but in Bernard's apartment in Brooklyn," he said. "There are some things I need to share with them if you would indulge me for just a little while longer," P.J. Foster continued.

Martin and Penny were not very pleased about relinquishing their children so soon after their return. But Elly, who normally never would have let Gabe out of her sight after the events of the last two days, urged them to reconsider and allow the children to spend some time with the professor and her uncle.

"Why don't we let Gabe and Alex get some well-deserved sleep tonight. We'll meet at my apartment tomorrow. Phinny and I have some catching up to do..."

"And some plans to make," the professor interrupted.

Chapter Twenty-Six

All Gabes Are Not Created Equal

It was at this meeting on Windsor Place in Brooklyn, New York, the next afternoon, when the almost teens consumed about the best chicken soup they had ever eaten, and where P.J. Foster began to reveal the missing pieces. There were secrets that had been kept in Jonas Foster's office at the American Museum of Natural History for the past thirty years, not in some sealed vault, but in an old worn duffel bag locked in an unsuspecting file cabinet.

In exchange for the information contained in these files, the professor exacted one and only one promise from Gabe and Alex. It was not that they would always follow their parents' advice, although that might be the prudent thing to do. It was not they would do their best in school, although that would be the expected thing to do. It was that they would be true to themselves in all they endeavored to do, no matter what challenge they might face.

"Can you make that promise, my dear children?" the professor asked hopefully.

"When will you tell us more? Alex asked as she glanced at Gabe.

"In due time you will learn it all, my young friends, and it will be up to you to decide whether or not to assist me with the work," he reassured them.

While the promise was a bit daunting to the two and the details yet to be revealed, they looked at each other, hesitated momentarily and then nodded in agreement.

"Does this involve a lot of reading?" Gabe asked.

"Will we get to travel to exotic places and investigate things?" Alex added.

Professor Foster smiled and gazed at Uncle Bernie when they heard the knock at the door. The children were startled by the apparent intrusion, their nerves a bit unraveled from yesterday's events.

"No need to worry, children. This visit is expected and will be brief," the professor informed them. Uncle Bernie opened the door, where Pete McDonough and Philip Kingsley Jr. stood, one holding a tattered duffel bag and the other a small brown paper wrapped package.

"It was easy enough to locate your duffel at the museum, Professor Foster," Pete said. "But it was no small feat finding the contents of this package," Philip interrupted. The professor thanked the two young men for their efforts and asked that they proceed with securing and dismantling the Westside underground lab.

The professor assured the children that it was never his intention to create computer clones of Gabe. "That was Kingsley's idea, and unfortunately I allowed him to convince me to go along with his plan, at least at first," the old man confessed. "He managed to keep me away from the lab with promises that the prototype would be destroyed once we could work directly with Gabe. I should have known better. Danielle warned me over and over again. I never made the connection between Kingsley and Julia. I was certain that wherever she vanished, she had finally abandoned her plans for revenge."

"So what were you planning to do with Gabe?" Alex asked.

"Yeah, exactly what were you going to do to me?" Gabe chimed in.

"Gabe, it was never what I was going to do to you. It was what I hoped you would do for yourself," the professor answered. "Bernard, please hand the bag to me."

"Phinny my dear friend, it would be just like you to keep your most valuable files in an old duffel bag," Uncle Bernie lovingly admonished his old mentor.

"Well you must admit, it is the last place anyone would look," the professor replied as he unzipped its main compartment. He removed several small cardboard boxes, each containing the prototype for one of his early inventions.

"Not very high tech by today's standards," he admitted to the children. "But I do have a flash drive or two in here, complements of my great granddaughter Danielle, with the data I've tracked on thousands of school children. And among these dog-eared yellowing hundred or so pages, are the plans for the next phase of the work, the so-called secret files that Kingsley tried to corrupt."

"Okay, now we're getting somewhere," Gabe exclaimed.

"Are we getting somewhere, Professor?" Alex asked a bit more tentatively.

"We are indeed, children! And I can tell you with complete certainty that none of this involves robot clones and brain reprogramming, or any sort of master race of almost teenagers. Those were the dreams, or should I say nightmarish visions, of a madman who might have had his way, if it wasn't for you."

"So what are your secret plans, Professor?" Gabe and Alex said in unison.

"They are not so much about changing children themselves," the old man replied.

"It never was about making children into something they were not, as I recall," Uncle Bernie added.

"You are quite right, Bernard. It took me a long time to understand that myself. The files reveal the hundreds of successes to date and offer the blueprint for us to proceed."

"Blueprint? Sounds like a plan to make clones of the perfect kid," Gabe said. "Well that's definitely not me. There is nothing about me that's perfect, so why make copies of me?"

"Actually, the files describe precisely the opposite plan, Gabe," the professor responded. And indeed, while no one is perfect, everyone is different. Kingsley never understood that and was convinced we could reprogram you and in turn any child who didn't quite fit our image of perfect."

"Then it's not about making copies of a better me?" Gabe asked.

"No, young man, because there is no better you. These past few days have confirmed decades of research in my files. You became a hero on your terms, not on anyone else's. And that's the task that awaits you and Alex, if you agree to join me."

"Join you in what exactly?" Gabe asked, still somewhat confused.

"Join me in finding the others, the children who are so convinced of their flaws that they have no idea that they are heroes," the professor responded.

160

"So Phinny, this is no longer about the tricks and gadgets?" Uncle Bernie asked.

"Well not entirely," the professor added with his characteristically mischievous smile. "It may take a gadget or two for some to discover their inner heroes. But that will make it all the more interesting!"

"So I take it we are about to resume our old partnership?" Uncle Bernie said.

"Indeed, my old friend. Wouldn't you agree that it's time to put the past behind us? There is no telling how much time either of us has left to finish what was started seventy years ago. What's more, Gabe and Alex have accomplished more in the last forty-eight hours to prove my theories than I could have done in as many years without them," the professor added, clearly directing his remarks to the two young heroes of the day.

"But wait, let's make it official," the professor said, as Uncle Bernie reached for the brown paper wrapped package.

"What is that, Uncle Bernie?" Gabe asked.

"Glad to see you're just a little bit curious about the contents of this package," Uncle Bernie responded.

"Let's just say I'm going to make it official, Gabe," the professor added. And with that disclosure, Gabe and Alex were handed their own Brooklyn Dodgers baseball caps, virtual replicas of the ones that P.J. Foster and Bernie Marshall had treasured since 1957.